IN

A CHIEF INSPECTOR

STO*h*Y

MORRISSEY MYSTERY

PLACES

KAY MITCHELL

W🌐RLDWIDE®

TORONTO • NEW YORK • LONDON
AMSTERDAM • PARIS • SYDNEY • HAMBURG
STOCKHOLM • ATHENS • TOKYO • MILAN
MADRID • WARSAW • BUDAPEST • AUCKLAND

IN STONY PLACES

A Worldwide Mystery/August 1993

First published by St. Martin's Press, Incorporated.

ISBN 0-373-26126-8

"I COULD HAVE KILLED HER IF I'D WANTED, RIGHT ON YOUR OWN SODDING DOORSTEP, MORRISSEY."

The chief inspector covered the mouthpiece. "Trace it!"

As Barrett moved at a trot out of the office, Morrissey took his hand away and forced his voice to take on neutrality, pushing the image of Katie away. Time enough for anger when the talking was done. He said, "I don't know what you're telling me."

The laugh that came back held no humor. "Oh, you bloody know, all right! Shall I tell you where I am, then, save the bother of tracing it?"

"Now listen..."

"No. *You* listen! Better watch it, Morrissey. That daughter of yours was lucky, but if I have to meet up with your wife sometime... Well, think about it. I wouldn't be that kind twice."

"...a sure and solid recommendation for any of those numerous mystery readers addicted to the genre."

—*Booklist*

For Mum

ONE

It was easier to stare out through the window than to face Gail, and anyway the flat dark clouds massing on the other side of the common offered a kind of kinship. Mood and weather black.

Black or bleak? Both.

Gail said, in the small voice she used when they quarrelled, 'The readers liked me', and flinched when the answer came sarcastically cutting.

'They liked your boobs. Why don't you stand on your head next time? I don't think they've tried that.'

'You could at least try... I'm getting nearly twice as much as last time.'

'Well, that's what it's all about. Money.'

'Look, I'll be late.'

'Fine. Better get a taxi; it's going to piss.'

Gail had a feeling of defeat. Where words were concerned, she usually lost. Strong on feelings, poor on intellect; Rob had told her that once, and it rankled.

She said, 'Well fine, fine. If money's such a dirty word, tell me about it when I'm rich.'

'I won't be here, my love.' The Carter twins were running back across the road with ice-cream faces. Inside the room Gail jerked her shoulders, sulky and upset. Without turning to look at her, Rob said, 'It's your life—your decision; live it the way you want. The choices are all down to you.'

Over the scrubby common, low cloud bellies, heavily pregnant with unshed rain, seemed almost to touch the highest part of the copse before it dipped out of sight behind a rise of ground. If Gail took the common path she would have to pass the trees, and the thought was disturbing.

'You won't make it to the other side without getting soaked.'

'I'll run.'

'That's stupid.'

'Yes, well, I'm a stupid person. You've just told me that.' With a sag-bag slung over her shoulder, Gail added edgily, 'I can't afford a taxi. See you tonight.'

When the rain came she was only half-way to the copse. It fell in great elephant tears, and a rumble of thunder threatened worse. She held her umbrella at an angle and kept her eyes fixed on the path, skidding on a loose stone and nearly losing her balance.

It was almost dark enough to be night—spooky-dark; and she never crossed the common at night; its emptiness frightened her. No, that was wrong, emptiness didn't worry her at all, it was rather what might be hidden in it, borrowing the shape of bush or tree.

A sharp flurry of rain pushed rattling against the stretched nylon of her umbrella, blowing cold against her legs. In the copse at the side of the path a twig snapped, incredibly loud in the silence, and brought a prickle of nervousness. A dog? It must be huge. She remembered that two Rottweilers exercised on the common regularly.

Holding the umbrella made her feel ungainly as she ran, and perhaps running was the wrong thing to do. It might make her seem more like prey. She could hear the animal's breath, loud and panting. Then she turned her head and found it wasn't a dog at all.

Looking into the darkness that lay behind the eyes, Gail knew bleak terror. She turned the umbrella like a shield, and had its flimsiness brushed aside without effort. It spun from her hand to be caught by the gusting breeze and bowled down the hill, cartwheeling and bouncing. From where she stood she could see the bus shelter, but not whether there were people in it. The urge to scream and the heaviness of fist were almost simultaneous.

THE EMPTY PATH straggled obliquely down from the copse to an old metal gate near the bus shelter, and out on to the minor road that skirted two small villages and half a dozen outlying farms. There was little traffic. For some reason the outside quietness made the couple waiting in the bus shelter mute their own voices, and the loudest sound was the increasing chatter of rain on the corrugated roof.

Lorraine was deep into her favourite subject, and Malcolm's eyes were becoming distant with boredom. To his way of thinking it ought to be enough for her that they were getting married, but instead she

went on about bridesmaids' dresses. He tried to close
his ears, but her voice still came through.

'I think apricot, don't you? A nice, soft apricot.
Your Tina'll look really pretty, and...' She broke off
in mid-sentence, scrubbing a peep-hole on a misted
pane. 'Did you hear that?'

'Somebody larking about.' Malcolm's hold on her
tightened uneasily.

'This weather?' She scrabbled in a pocket for a tissue to clear a bigger patch of window. 'It sounded...'

'Like somebody larking about.' And, to take her
mind off it, 'What about blue? I've always liked
blue.'

Half reluctantly she turned her dark eyes back to
him, and let herself be diverted. 'Cornflower or
royal?'

He fumbled; for him, blue was blue. 'Sort of pale,
you know, like that jumper you bought last week.'

'Suppose so.' Humouring, because she'd already
decided on apricot.

Through the cleared glass the black umbrella
bowling down the hill caught her eye. At first Lorraine thought it was an empty dustbin liner, then her
eyes recognised the roundness. 'That's funny! Somebody's lost an umbrella.' She craned her neck. 'Can't
see anybody coming after it.'

'Funny.'

Together they watched the freshening wind spin it
towards them.

The sky was now a uniform grey.

'Looks like the rain's set in,' Malcolm said. 'If I got that umbrella, we could make a dash for it.'

'Somebody'll be bound to come after it.'

'Give it five minutes, then.'

They waited. When the common stayed empty, Lorraine suggested, 'We could always hand it in. It wouldn't be as if we were stealing it, would it?'

The umbrella had come to rest against the bottom of the hedge, and the long, wet grass soaked Malcolm's trouser-bottoms. When he shook it free of rain he saw it was almost new. He stared from the umbrella to the copse. Supposing that scream had been for real. Shouldn't he find out? Feeling foolish, he moved away from the hedge.

From inside the bus shelter, Lorraine saw him begin to walk up the hill, and went out into the rain. 'Mal, come on, hurry up!' Relieved when he turned back, she hung on to his arm. 'Daft!'

'I thought I ought to...'

'I know you did. You said yourself—larking about. No point getting wet though, is there?' She began to pull him down the street. It couldn't be anything else in broad daylight. She settled her mind into comfortable prejudice.

Bad things didn't happen to nice girls.

THE CALL was logged in at Malminster police station at four-twenty, and it took only three minutes for a Panda car to pull up near the bus shelter in Mortimer Road. The rain had stopped half an hour ago and a strengthening sun was starting to punch holes in the leaden sky.

On the rise near the copse a man with a white bull terrier had been waiting uneasily, the dog whining by his side. When Police Constable Hicks came breathily up from the patrol car he knew it was no prank call; the look on the ageing, once florid, face said that. He didn't even get the chance to ask questions before he was bundled towards the copse. The dog at their feet tried a half-hearted growl.

Its owner, bronchitically staccato, said, 'Wooster found her lying just inside the trees. Damn dog, thought he was after rabbits when he went in. Wasn't, unfortunately. Wish I hadn't looked.'

Hicks freed his arm. 'I'd better have a look myself then, sir.'

The PC cherished dreams of fast promotion, and he took care where he put his feet. The girl was lying on her face half-hidden by undergrowth, arms spread. Automatically he bent to feel for a pulse, recoiling from the cold skin. His first corpse. As he reached for his two-way radio his knees suddenly felt loose, and he began to sweat.

He thought with unwanted understanding that this was what the old man must be feeling like.

TWO

MORRISSEY HAD LEFT his office in a hurry, having belatedly realised why Margaret had given him so many funny looks at breakfast. Thank God for the florist on the corner! Red roses and dinner at that Italian place she liked might square him.

Over the past few months his marriage seemed to have settled into a quiet phase, and he found himself liking domestic felicity. Not that he blamed Margaret for the bumpy patches; marriage to a policeman meant too many spoiled dinners, too many cancelled outings, and Margaret's temper wasn't exactly saintly. Come to that, neither was his own.

That afternoon's downpour had given way to patchy sunlight, the thick, thundery atmosphere had gone and in its place there was a cooler freshness. Even here, in the middle of the city, the air for once smelled clean, and he took his time walking back along the rain-washed pavement.

Whistling tunelessly, the roses chosen, paid for and sent on their way, he went back to the police building. The heavy swing doors let out a burst of hot, dry air. The ventilation system never worked properly, and now they'd put new windows in that didn't open wide enough for a sparrow to spit through.

He'd intended to ring Florio's as soon as he got back in his office, but one look at Barrett's face told him there would be no point. The new file on his desk had a red sticker, and red stickers didn't mean early nights. He sighed.

'Where?'

'West Common. And Sir rang a couple of minutes ago; wants to talk to you later. He seemed a bit hung out.'

'I know why. He's anticipating the pasting we'll get in the papers, and he's already squirming.' The anger Morrissey felt was familiar and made worse by a niggling sense of impotence. He knew what waited on the common, knew how painstaking would be the hunt for even the smallest piece of evidence, but he knew too that where this random killer was concerned what they had to hope for most desperately was one small mistake. He skimmed the brief report.

Grimacing at Barrett, he reached out a hand towards the telephone. 'Give me two minutes, Neil. I have to make peace.' As the door closed, he heard Margaret's voice in his ear.

Barrett sat in the car and waited. Better to marry than to burn, eh? He himself felt no inclination yet to follow St Paul's advice; his philosophy of better a fast burn than a slow roast was one he had developed for himself.

Morrissey's stony face was unreadable when he got into the passenger seat, and as Barrett moved the car smoothly away he knew better than to ask what Margaret had said.

They pulled up in Mortimer Road behind Hicks's Panda. An elderly man was sitting in its back seat, and the bull terrier at his side bared threatening teeth when Barrett looked in.

Waiting at the top of the rise, the PC watched their coming with a mixture of relief and envy. Once they took over, there would be nothing left for him to do but make out a report sheet. And probably drive the old man home.

He brought his hand up in a regulation salute; someone had once told him the fastest way out of uniform division was to get yourself noticed, and now was as good a time as any.

Morrissey nodded, and a faint smile touched his face. 'Who have you got in the car?'

'It was his dog that found the body, sir. When I got here, he looked like he was going to pass out; I thought it best to get him sat down.'

'Asked him any questions?'

'I asked if he'd seen anybody, but he said the common was empty except for him and the dog.'

Morrissey squatted in the wet grass and old leaves. Impossible to guess what the dead woman looked like from the face down position she was lying in, but equally impossible to move her until the photographer had done his job.

Knowing that didn't stop an instinctive wish to turn her face from the muddy ground. The long, silky soft hair suggested youth. How young? Eighteen? Twenty? Katie was eighteen. And Katie walked home alone. He tried to push his daughter from his mind. At home he was a father; here, the best thing he could do for her, and every other woman in Malminster, was to keep his mind unclogged.

There was a tear in the dead girl's shiny black raincoat where it had snagged on a low branch, and her shoes had fallen off as she was dragged out of sight.

He stepped carefully back out of the undergrowth and stood with Hicks and Barrett on the path.

'I suppose you got your witness's name and address?' he asked Hicks.

'Yes, sir. A Mr Charles Hodgson, 18 Grasmere Crescent. Retired accountant.'

'In a minute or two you can run him home.' He looked at Barrett. 'Go down and see if Mr Hodgson has anything useful to contribute, will you?' Hicks made to follow, but Morrissey called him back. More cars and a police van arrived. 'I'd like a copy of your report on my desk first thing in the morning.'

'Yes, sir.'

'Bring it in yourself, will you,' he added, and watched Hicks struggle to decide if the request meant a compliment or foreshadowed a reprimand.

BARRETT THOUGHT HE recognised the girl. He'd said so when the pathologist turned her over. But where and when had stayed elusive until now.

Morrissey had brought him to the clammy cold mortuary. It wasn't his first visit, and he didn't like it any better than he had the first time. The dead girl's clothing had been sent for forensic examination, and her body, its marks and bruises photographed, waited now for a post-mortem.

The night attendant was crass, pulling down the sheet with a leer. 'Bloody waste! I could have fancied that.'

Morrissey looked at him with distaste and moved the girl's head gently, looking at the mottled bruising on her face and the deep indentation about the neck. It hadn't been an easy way to die.

The pathologist had said some time between twelve and two. The common would have been empty then, swept bare of strollers by the heavy rain. What would have made her choose to take that particular path at that particular time?

'Page three,' Barrett said abruptly. Morrissey eyed him. 'That's where I've seen her. Page three in the *Sun*. Last week sometime.' Then as Morrissey's eyes stayed on him, he explained defensively, 'There was a copy lying about in the locker-room. I don't buy it myself.'

It was the kind of remark that would normally have made the chief inspector smile; but not now.

The attendant's nasal drone irritated them both. Even when what he said was, on the surface, helpful. 'Bet you won't guess how lucky you two are tonight,

I still got all last week's pictures.' He dropped the sheet back over the body, and moved off.

They followed down a stump of corridor into a grubby cubby-hole that held a stained table and chair. Thumb-tacked to one wall was a row of roughly cut out page three girls.

He laughed as though the whole thing was funny. 'Never thought I'd get one of 'em in there. Right good close-up that's been.'

Barrett's anger spiralled; he forced his attention to the wall. 'This one,' he said tersely, taking out drawing-pins.

'You can't have it. I want to show it round me mates.'

'You'll get it back. In the fullness of time.'

'Oh yeah, I don't doubt. Won't do me much good in six months though, will it? I shouldn't have said nothing.'

'Don't worry,' Barrett said wearily. 'They'll probably print it in colour next week.'

Puffy eyes brightened. 'Think so?'

'That's what it's all about, isn't it?'

Morrissey caught the look of calculation. He barked, 'This stays confidential. Mention it to anyone, and I'll charge you with obstruction.'

'It's my bloody cut-out!'

'And it'll be your three months' holiday.'

They left him sullenly staring at the empty wall space.

'Think he'll take any notice?' Barrett said when they were back in the car.

Morrissey said, 'I almost hope he doesn't.'

GAIL LATIMER WAS identified by her flatmate at ten that night. Morrissey took the girl back to his office and tried to be gentle.

'We need to know about how she spent her time, where she went, and especially the men she knew. Was there any one man in particular?'

Susan Reed was more angular than curvy, with long brown hair caught hastily back and beginning to escape. She looked likely to faint as she shook her head, and he wished the tea he had asked for would come.

'She was a good-looking girl,' Barrett said. 'I would have thought...'

'That she would have had more than one man in tow. That's what you were going to say, isn't it? Well, she hadn't. Gail wasn't that sort of person.' Susan was shaking slightly and abruptly folded her arms across her breasts, hands gripping her shoulders.

'Could she have arranged to meet anyone on the common?' Morrissey asked.

'No.'

There was no hesitation and he wondered at her certainty, but let it go when tea arrived, leaving her in peace while she drank, hands clasped tight about the cup. When colour came back to her face, he tried again. 'Sometimes the smallest, most unlikely thing helps,' he said, and wondered why her eyes made him uncomfortable. 'That's why we need to know everything about her, even if you think it's intrusive.'

'I know that. I don't need it explaining.' She put the cup down and sat up straight. 'Most murderers are known to their victims. That's what you're working on, isn't it? Well, not Gail.'

'You knew her that well? How long had you shared the flat?'

'Two years. I was—very fond of her. We confided more than what you probably call girl-talk, and yes, I did know her well. Well enough to know if she were having problems with a man.'

'Can you give me her parents' address? I'd like to break the news as quickly as possible rather than have them hear it second-hand.'

'She had none. There's a married brother in Manchester; they weren't all that close, he's about ten years older. I can give you his address. Oh God!' Susan stared at her restless hands. 'It's all wrong, sitting here talking and drinking tea—I feel so bloody numb, as if it isn't happening.'

'Are you nervous about going back to the flat? Is there somewhere you'd rather go, or anyone you want to have stay?'

'No, I'll be fine. Thanks, but I'm not nervous, not about that.'

'What, then?'

She weighed them up. Morrissey wondered if they would be found wanting. Then she said, 'It's the emptiness I'll find tomorrow, and the next day, and the next. Probably I'll move.'

'We'll need to look through her things,' he said abruptly. 'When you feel able.' Odd how awkward he felt with this girl.

At least she didn't say what she was probably thinking: that he didn't really believe she knew everything about her dead flatmate; that somewhere among Gail's belongings was something that might point to a man.

Instead, she said, 'Whenever you like.'

And waited for him to decide.

THREE

IT WAS almost midnight when Morrissey got home. Upstairs, in the darkened bedroom, Margaret watched the headlights of his car cut a bright sweep as he came up the drive, and turned over, her back to the door.

She wasn't sulking, she wasn't feeling hurt; she was just... And there she gave up, because she didn't know the word to use for what she felt. Perhaps something like an ant buried by a constant trickle of sand.

The roses were in a vase on the low table in the living-room; near them was her present to him, carefully searched for, carefully wrapped. He would find it himself either tonight or tomorrow; it didn't matter now. Another anniversary had ended.

The headlights went out and she lay stiffly waiting for the sound of his key in the front door. When it came, part of her, perversely, wanted to get up and go to him, to hear relief in his quiet 'Margaret?'

Morrissey stood in the silent hall. The living-room light was on, and he knew there would be sandwiches and a thermos of coffee. Tonight of all nights they would be a tangible reproach. Evidence, if he needed it, that Margaret was a good wife, while he...?

Damn it, she knew these things came with the job.

Then he went in and saw the roses; and at the same time the ribboned package. Another accusation.

Deserved.

He couldn't blame the job for his forgetting; it had been blind carelessness. Not intentional, maybe, but lack of intent didn't lessen the crime. Marriages had foundered on less.

He left the package alone until he had cleared away the remains of his solitary supper. Then when he could avoid it no longer he tore off the wrappings.

Dylan Thomas, *Portrait of the Artist as a Young Dog*. Morrissey turned the book over in his hands, knowing how Margaret must have hunted to find this first edition. No last-minute dash to the shop on the corner. Illogically he resented her remembering when he forgot. He carried it to the shelf and put it between *Death and Entrances* and *The Map of Love*, turned off the light and went quietly upstairs.

Katie's door was open and the landing light fell on her face. The memory of Gail Latimer in the rain-drenched copse came to his mind. Not much difference in age. Katie sometimes walked across the common, too. His daughter was no safer than any man's. In the room across the landing his son was snoring softly, arms flung out, the duvet half on the floor. As Morrissey lifted it back into place, Mike half-woke, and then almost immediately began the gentle snoring again.

In their bedroom Margaret lay silent and unmoving. He undressed quietly, trying not to disturb her, and slid into bed. When the regular pattern of his breathing showed he was asleep, she went downstairs to heat a cup of milk and take two aspirin.

IT WAS barely eight when he reached his office. Margaret had overslept, and he had taken her a cup of tea, relieved that any recriminations would have to be shelved until later.

Hicks was already waiting with a freshly pressed look, and Morrissey forced his mind back to the work on hand. He added the PC's report to the Latimer file, and nodded.

'Good bit of writing. Nice to read a clear report.'

Hicks, who had sat uneasily while the chief inspector read, shifted forward alertly. 'Thank you, sir.'

Unsmiling, Morrissey held the PC's eyes, and approved the way they met his without needing to shift away. 'Right. I'll put in a good word. Off you go, then.'

When the door closed, Barrett said, 'Another eager beaver.'

'We need 'em,' Morrissey pointed out. 'The more there are, the less leg-work for us.' He picked up the file and levered himself out of his chair. 'Come on then damn it; the day's half over. If you get the car round, we'll have another talk with Susan Reed.'

Barrett didn't argue; he knew Morrissey well enough to recognise a bad case of frustration. Things obviously hadn't gone well at home last night. He also knew better than to ask.

The flat was ground-floor and on the far side of the common. Looking out through the old-fashioned sash window, Morrissey could see part of the path. And there were attics; in this house and in the six or seven adjoining. Anyone looking out of a high window could have seen someone lurking among the trees.

The dark shadows under Susan Reed's eyes suggested a sleepless night. Probably Gail's brother was looking the same. It would have been well after midnight when the Manchester police broke the news.

He turned from the window and joined Barrett in the bedroom. There were twin beds with flower-bright duvets.

'You shared the bedroom, then?' he asked. 'Not separate rooms?'

'It's a one-bedroom flat,' Susan said, and watched Barrett open drawers. Morrissey guessed she had spent the night on the living-room settee, and wondered how long it would be before the uneasiness left her and she could take possession of her bed again.

It bothered him to turn belongings over; prying into private, secret things. But there was always the chance, even when it seemed least likely, that something might point the way. Instinctively he knew that wouldn't happen this time, but the rules demanded he look.

Susan leaned against the door frame, dark eyes empty. Barrett found a proof of the page three photograph.

She said, 'It was out of character, but you wouldn't believe how much more money she got from that than straight modelling. Stupid, isn't it? Tits and bums. Bloody stupid!' She turned away, and a minute later they heard her filling the kettle in the kitchen. Barrett looked sheepish.

'What about Gail? Did it worry her, that kind of work?' Morrissey went to stand in the kitchen doorway. 'Upset her?'

Susan shrugged. 'The money made up for it. Or it would have if she'd had time to spend it.'

'And you?' he said. 'You model, too?'

She flushed, and he got the impression it was more anger than embarrassment. 'No,' she said shortly. 'I work in graphic design.'

'Did Gail know you disapproved?'

'I haven't said I did.'

'Not in so many words, but some things don't need words, do they?'

'I think it's exploitative. A lot of women think that, you know.' Her eyes accused him.

'Surprisingly, some men agree; but you know that too, of course.'

'Not enough to count.' She turned away abruptly. 'I'm going to make coffee; would you like some?'

'Thanks. Both black.'

She filled three mugs, Barrett came in with a diary and put the small, blue, leather-backed book on the table. 'You said no boyfriend,' he observed. 'Although diaries are private things, so there's no reason why you should have seen this.'

Susan stared at the table; coffee slopped. 'Damn.' She reached for a paper towel. 'What would I have found if I had?' she asked, wiping the table.

'A lot about someone called Rob, who wasn't pleased about the photograph,' Morrissey said.

'Oh.'

'You don't know him?'

'Gail didn't discuss any man with me, and I didn't pry into her diary.'

It was an expected response, but Morrissey still felt an edge of disappointment.

'I'm sorry,' she said, 'but is it that important?'

'It would be useful to eliminate him from our enquiries.'

'I suppose so.' Her voice, like her eyes, was expressionless.

'She must have known him well,' said Barrett. He put an estate-agent's leaflet in front of her. 'I found this, too. If you look, you'll see it's been written on.'

She stared at the rough heart-shape drawn around the sepia photograph of a house. Underneath, the words, 'Rob and Gail. Their house.'

'It looks as though she was making plans,' Morrissey said. 'And it makes me wonder why she was being so secretive, and why she didn't tell you about it.

Why do you think that was, when you were such close friends?'

She gripped the table. 'I don't know. I can't tell you why.'

There was a terrible pain in her eyes, and Morrissey wondered what she was holding back. Whatever it was, he would have to dig for it, bit by bit, because it was plain that Susan Reed wouldn't tell him voluntarily.

FOUR

'WELL, AT LEAST we've got a lead,' Barrett said as they walked. 'Something she was keeping secret. Rob. Could be Robert. Worth checking with the other files.'

'Mm.'

'Maybe he gets to know them first, then does a permanent ditching when they get too fond.' He squinted at Morrissey's set face. 'What do you think?'

'I wish I thought it would be that easy.'

Barrett fell silent; he hadn't suggested it was going to be easy. What he had suggested was that it was worth checking whether 'Rob' had a place in the lives of the other two dead girls. And at least it was a positive approach. Resentment smouldered. When he was chief inspector... He dreamed dreams.

Under the trees in the copse the ground was still spongy, and old leaves clung to their shoes like dead fingers. Morrissey couldn't have said why he had come back; there would be nothing to find; the scene of crime team had been over the whole area. But something bothered him, and he didn't know what. Moodily he scuffed around. His brown brogues, thick soled, turned up their noses at the damp ground, but

Barrett's polished black acquired an inch-deep tide-mark. He lifted one foot to look at the damage and scowled at Morrissey's back.

If he'd known they'd be tramping in the under-growth, he'd have worn wellies; they were in the car boot. Something else to feel disgruntled about. Self-righteously he decided that whatever the quarrel had been about, he was on the side of Morrissey's wife.

The chief inspector glanced round and caught him balanced on one foot. 'Should have put your wellies on,' he said dismissively.

Barrett let his foot drop. *Shit!*

On the far side of the copse, furthest from the path, the ground fell away under scrubby gorse and coarse long grass to where Mortimer Road circled round the edge of the common before turning off towards the villages of Norton and Manorfield.

Morrissey stood on the edge of the trees and looked across the road at the crescent of houses, built just after the war; a secluded group, well screened and up-market—or at least that's what the people who lived there thought. Morrissey could remember his father dismissing them with a curt 'Jerry built!' when they first went up.

The bull terrier that had sniffed out Gail Latimer's body lived with its owner in one of them; another had a For Sale sign in its garden, and Morrissey recog-nised it with a start. There had been no address on the estate-agent's leaflet Barrett had found in the girl's bedroom, just a photograph and a description of a house and its accommodation, but Morrissey was in no doubt that it was the house he was looking at now. He pointed it out to Barrett.

'Might as well cut across,' he said, and set off over the bumpy-rough tussocks. Barrett followed, cursing under his breath.

The woman who opened the door was suspicious, leaving the security chain in place until she saw Morrissey's warrant card. Sensible, he thought. If he were female, with a murderer on the loose, he'd be wary too. He showed her Gail's photograph.

She said, 'There's already been a policeman asking about that. I told him I didn't know her.'

Morrissey said patiently, 'I know, but this is a different question. I think she may have been to look round your house. Possibly with a man.'

Her eyes went large and startled as though the thought of it violated her safety. 'You mean the man who...' She couldn't finish it and her voice trailed off.

'We don't know,' Morrissey said. 'But if you could remember anything?'

She took the photograph and studied it carefully this time. 'Her face is a bit familiar,' she admitted. 'She was a pretty thing, wasn't she? But I see so many people, and if she lived near the common I might have seen her anywhere. I don't really remember her coming here. But Brian might have seen her instead. Brian's my husband,' she said when Morrissey's eyebrows twitched upwards. 'If they came at the weekend, I wouldn't have known. I work at the hospital

Saturday and Sunday, and it would have been Brian who showed them round.'

'He isn't at home now?'

'No. Not until six.' She looked doubtful. 'I suppose you're going to ask me where he works?'

Morrissey nodded. 'If you wouldn't mind; it would be a help. If he remembers her.'

She confided suddenly. 'My daughter lives in Cheshire now. She was at Bradford University when the Ripper...' Her voice trailed off again. 'I was so bloody worried,' she said in a sudden burst of anger. 'And now it's all starting again. Of course I'll tell you where to find Brian. He's the sales manager at Crowther's Biscuits. Brian Appleby.' She handed back the photograph. 'I'll give him a ring and tell him you're coming.'

Morrissey nodded. 'I'm grateful for your help.' She smiled at him uncertainly, and as he and Barrett turned away he heard the door being locked behind them.

'Bit of luck that,' Barrett said as they began to walk back to the car. 'Saves on a trip to the estate-agent's.'

'That it doesn't,' said the chief inspector tersely. 'I want to know everyone who showed any interest in that house at all. When we've been to Crowther's, see it as your next job.'

Barrett said nothing; in fact he said nothing all the way to Crowther's, but if Morrissey picked up that his sergeant was being distant, he didn't let on.

There was a stale tobacco smell. That was the first thing Morrissey noticed, and even the keen draught of air through the partly open window couldn't dispel it. Appleby's office was comfortable and well used; nothing flashy and new. Obviously the firm believed in keeping costs down, and that was a good sign as far as Morrissey was concerned. The man himself was expecting them; his wife had been as good as her word. He gave the photograph careful scrutiny.

'Of course the agents will have her on file if she did come to have a look round,' he said. He set the photograph on the desk in front of him and shifted his weight forward, leaning on both elbows. 'I think I remember her. If it's the girl I'm thinking of, she came alone, Sunday afternoon about two weeks ago. Dreamy, full of enthusiasm. You'd have thought she was going to rush back to the agents and pay for it there and then. I asked about her fiancé, but she changed the subject.'

'Didn't mention his name at all?'

'Not that I remember. Nor did she tell me where she lived. I gather from the news that it was somewhere near the common?'

'Not far from where you are, really,' Morrissey said. 'You might even have seen her from time to time, walking across.'

'We don't use the common much any more; not with the children grown and gone.'

'Your wife mentioned you had a daughter.'

'Two,' he said, and didn't elaborate.

Barrett butted in. 'You haven't seen the girl anywhere else then, sir? The girl in the photograph.
Apart from thinking she might have come to look
round your house one Sunday afternoon, you've
never seen her before.'

'Never,' Appleby said easily. 'I thought I'd already established that with the chief inspector.'

'You did,' Barrett said. 'Sometimes I'm a bit ob-
tuse. Can I ask what daily paper you read?' Morrissey gave him a sharp look.

'The *Telegraph*. It has a good crossword.'

'And at the office?' Barrett persisted. 'Do you get
another one to read at lunchtime, maybe? Something lighter?'

Shifting in his chair Appleby said, 'Sometimes.'

'Much lighter? The *Sun*, perhaps?'

Morrissey thought Appleby was going to deny it
before the man's eyes followed Barrett's to the waste
bin, hidden from where the chief inspector sat. Then
Barrett got off his chair and reached forward. 'Yesterday's,' he said, shaking it open. 'Did you get last
Wednesday's too?'

Morrissey gave Barrett a look of satisfaction.

The sergeant said, 'By the way, just for the record,
sir, could you give me your full name?' He opened his
notebook.

'Appleby,' the sales manager said uneasily. 'Brian
Robert Appleby.'

FIVE

'I THINK WE SHOULD have been a bit harder on him,' Barrett said as they left the biscuit company's offices.

'He's not going anywhere,' Morrissey said mildly. 'Besides, in a town the size of Malminster, how many men do you think read the *Sun*?' Barrett didn't reply. 'And a hell of a lot will be called Robert. Popular name.'

'But this one had met the girl,' Barrett argued. 'Knowledge and opportunity.'

Morrissey sighed, and wished Barrett would learn not to be so eager to chase the first hare. 'Let's see if he had knowledge and opportunity with the first two before we hang him,' he suggested. 'It'll save a public apology.' He got into the car. 'Drop me at the office while you sort out that list of viewers. I haven't been upstairs to see the chief superintendent yet; he'll be turning from simmer to boil.'

This reminder that Morrissey too got prodded from above was soothing as Barrett drove out of the industrial estate and turned on to the Middlebrook Road. Above the launderette in the parade of shops, the maisonette was empty, its bare windows accusing.

Morrissey saw the quick upward glance. Conscience, he hoped, considering that Barrett's interest in David Pace's wife had been the prime reason for the CID Aide asking for transfer. It rankled that Malminster's loss had been Lincoln's gain; Pace would have made a good DC.

Barrett dropped the chief inspector outside the police station's main entrance. Morrissey went in through the swing doors and took the stairs two at a time, his long legs hardly noticing. He was thinking about Appleby and how much it would improve the climate if he could tell Osgodby they had a lead, however tenuous. It was that thought that made him put off going up to the chief superintendent's office a little longer.

On the chief inspector's desk a recently installed computer terminal sat in squat promise of efficiency. Morrissey's son Mike had been impressed to learn that his father wasn't considered too old to learn its intricacies. But then Mike, like most fourteen-year-olds, considered anyone over twenty-five had one foot in the grave.

Morrissey accessed the file on Susan Howarth, the first of the murdered girls, a twenty-year-old assistant in a tobacconist's shop. To the names Appleby, Rob, Robert or Robin, the computer gave him the same response—*Sorry no information*. He tried the name of Crowther's Biscuits. Nothing. Damn it, it wasn't any faster than reading through the file himself. Disgruntled, he began again with the second file.

Obliquely the thought came that it could be counted an immortality of sorts to be lodged for ever in a computer memory bank. He reflected that it wasn't much consolation for what went before. Immortality always had snags.

The second victim had been Diane Anderson, a twenty-two-year-old typist working for the Redfearn Agency. Among the names of clients listed by the agency he saw Crowther's Biscuits. Last year she had temped for them. A hair from which to suspend a sword; slender, but perhaps enough.

Osgodby seemed to think so as he leaped on it. He said, 'Don't think I'm going to ask if you believe there's anything in it, John, because I'm not; I don't want to risk getting a negative. It's enough that when the chief constable jumps on my back I can say we have a strong lead.' He sucked on his teeth. 'Bringing Appleby in, then?'

'Not yet,' Morrissey said cautiously.

'Thought you might say that,' Osgodby replied. 'Must be developing some of that sixth sense you're famous for. Let me know when anything happens.'

Barrett was at his desk when Morrissey went back downstairs. He looked disgruntled, and more so when the chief inspector said dismissively, 'That was quick.'

'It's getting to the point where everything's on computers. Push a button and get a printout. Magic. We're being taken over by machines.'

'What you really mean,' said Morrissey knowingly, 'is that you hadn't time to assess the talent,' and he grinned when Barrett grumpily slapped a list of names and addresses on his desk.

'Gail Latimer went in alone,' the sergeant said. 'Spoils things a bit. I mean, if she already knew it was Appleby's house, why bother with a permit to view?'

'Living dangerously?' suggested Morrissey. 'Putting a bit of pressure on? You'll notice she went to look round when Mrs. Appleby wasn't there.'

'Then you think it's him?' Barrett's surprise was almost childlike, and Morrissey winced.

'No,' he said, 'I don't mean that at all. I'm showing how easy it is to build up circumstantial evidence without a shred of anything that would pass for proof.' The sergeant's face grew expressionless. Morrissey gave him a crumb. 'But there is a link between Crowther's and Diane Anderson. She did some temping for them. See what you can find out about it from Redfearn's and then we'll talk to Appleby again. If we rattle him enough and he's guilty, it'll show.'

Barrett picked up his jacket and went out again. Morrissey hugged the telephone receiver to his ear and tried his home number. The monotonous ringing tone sounded loud. Eventually he gave up.

A constable brought in two fax sheets. They were unhelpful. The Met had learned nothing useful from the *Sun* offices at Wapping, and the second fax, from the Manchester police, showed that the agency handling Gail's modelling career was both reputable and squeaky clean. But she was only a name on their books. Reliable, could have done well if she'd been given time. But time had been arbitrarily taken away from her.

The picture that was now building in Morrissey's mind didn't fit Appleby. Appleby was married, he had children, his life was a success—and it didn't fit at all. He talked on the telephone for a long time to the police psychiatrist. When he'd finished, he still had more questions than answers. Impotent! How the blazes was he expected to know if Appleby couldn't get it up any more?

It was almost one o'clock when Barrett came back. Morrissey had already lunched on indifferent steak pie that sat heavy. He warned the sergeant it was lethal. 'Whatever you have,' he said, 'get it down fast. I want to get back to Crowther's.'

Barrett reached into his pocket. 'Want my notebook?' The chief inspector shook his head. 'Let it keep until you've eaten. I can't decipher that spider's crawl of yours.'

Morrissey dialled his home number again and still got no answer. Funny how silence could be both a solace and a punishment.

Then Gail Latimer's brother arrived, and Morrissey had him brought up to the office. The man looked unhealthily pale, his pupils over-bright. Mousy-fair hair was already beginning to recede from his temples, and when he sat down in front of Morrissey's desk and dropped his head on his hands, the chief inspector saw a near-bald patch at the back of his head.

Susan Reed had said the brother and sister weren't all that close, but this man looked shattered and sleepless as he said, 'I couldn't come sooner. Work. I had to wait for somebody to cover.'

'What kind of work?'

'Gas-fitter. I'm supposed to be on emergency call-out. I suppose it looks bad, not coming straight over, but I couldn't.'

'It wouldn't have changed anything if you had. I'm sorry about your sister. How long is it since you saw her?'

'Couple of months. You're sure it's Gail?'

There was a tenuous hope in the question, but Morrissey had to kill it. 'I'm sure; she was identified by her flatmate. And now that you're here, I'll have to ask you to identify her too as next of kin.'

Latimer burst out. 'It's so bloody stupid! Things were just starting to come right for her, and now this. Bloody stupid!' He looked bewildered.

'Starting to come right?' said Morrissey. 'Modelling, you mean.'

'Everything. We were getting to know each other again. I thought, we both thought, there was plenty of time.'

'But she was your sister,' Morrissey said. 'Why did you need to get to know her?'

'Different foster homes. I thought you'd know that. We only found each other again two years back. You'd be surprised how reticent social services can be.'

'No, I wouldn't,' said Morrissey with past knowledge. 'What about her foster family, then. Where do
they live?'

Latimer said, 'Malminster. Why else would she be
living here?'

Why else indeed, thought Morrissey, and wondered why, if she and Gail had been so close, Susan
Reed hadn't known about foster parents. Or had
she—and just chosen not to tell?

He asked, 'Did she still see much of them?'

'Not if she could help it. She moved out at sixteen,
and wouldn't go back. I don't know what it was all
about; Gail hadn't told me properly. She said she'd
been locked in a cupboard if she didn't behave. She'd
moved away before I found her or I'd have sorted
them out.'

'And how did you find her, finally?'

Latimer grimaced. 'I got good mates with one of
your lot, good bloke. He pulled more weight than me.
I should've made her move to Manchester straight
off, live with us. She'd have been all right then.'

'But you couldn't have known,' said Morrissey.
'And if you had, you'd have prevented it. There's
nothing to blame yourself for.'

'Is that right?' Latimer's tone was bitter. 'Bloody
good brother I've been, haven't I?'

But it was always the same with death; guilt pour-
ing in for things not done. 'This foster family she was
with,' Morrissey said. 'Can you give me their address?'

'Yeah, I wrote it out, just in case.' He took a folded paper from his pocket and handed it across the desk. 'I went to look at the place once; Gail never knew. Looks all right from the outside. Didn't see them, though.'

Morrissey recognised the address. It was one of the newer private estates that had been built during the housing boom fifteen years back. Low-priced housing taken up by blue-collar workers. He put the slip of paper on his desk. 'I'll have to pay them a visit, even if it's only a formality,' he said.

'Have a good look while you're there,' Latimer suggested. 'I know there was a lot Gail still had to tell me.' He drew himself up straight on the chair, his knuckles white where he gripped the sides. 'I think I'd like to see her now and get it over with.'

'Just one more question: did she mention the name Rob?'

'Rob? No, I don't think she ever did. Is it important?'

'Probably not.' The chief inspector put the foster family's address in his pocket and got up from his chair. 'I'll find someone to take you to the mortuary,' he said, and left Latimer staring at the wall.

In the outer office DC Smythe was on his own, doing slow two-finger typing. He seemed happy to leave it to escort Latimer.

Morrissey said, 'When it's over, bring him back and look after him in the canteen. He looks as if he needs something inside him. I'll want to see him again before he leaves.' Downstairs, in the information room, WPC Janet Yarby was using the main computer. The chief inspector handed her the foster parents' address and watched her feed in the information, wondering if Barrett's secret passion was still as strong. Time was when he couldn't be prised away, but WPC seemed to have a persuasive way of saying no.

The printer chattered, and she brought the sheet to him. 'Nothing recent,' she said, 'and nothing in Malminster, but there's an old indecent assault from way back, in the Leeds area, nineteen seventy-two.'

Morrissey took the printout upstairs. Was that why Gail had been so eager to get away? The thought came that police work could resemble working in a sewer.

Barrett was waiting for him. 'Are we...'

'Yes, we are,' Morrissey snapped in sudden and impotent anger. 'What did you get from Redfearn's?'

Wondering what he was supposed to have done wrong, the sergeant said, 'Only that Diane had asked to be moved from the job.' He met the chief inspector's scowl with innocent eyes and concealed satisfaction. 'Sexual harassment, only she refused to name the man who was pestering her. That's what it says in the personnel file, anyway.'

'Does it now?' said Morrissey gently. 'Does it indeed?'

SIX

APPLEBY WASN'T THERE. His secretary said he was
giving a pep talk to some of the sales reps, and
wouldn't be back until the next day.

Morrissey eyed her. She was giving off an air of
brisk efficiency and looked too young to get away
with it. He suspected that was why her hair had been
pulled back so firmly. If she let its owl-brown curls
fall loose, she'd look like a schoolgirl. He asked, 'Is
it the usual thing for him to go to them and not the
other way round, Miss er...?'

'Karen Breen.' She smiled. 'Why not? It gets his
bum off the chair for a bit. I wish I could go with
him.'

'What about yesterday, with all that rain? I suppose that would keep him in where it was warm and
dry.'

'You don't get wet when you have a car,' she said,
'But yes, he was in the office all day.'

'Didn't go out at all?'

'Only for lunch.'

'And what time would that be?'

'I don't know. I went earlish, about half-past
twelve, and he wasn't here when I got back, thank

heaven.' Morrissey's eyebrows twitched. She confided. 'I was late.'

'And Mr Appleby came back at . . . ?'

'Half-past two. He came back with Ken Fields from accounts, and they were shut up in his office until after three.'

Barrett said, 'I suppose he keeps a diary, when he's in and when he's out. That sort of thing.'

'Not always, not for every minute.'

'So you wouldn't know where he was on a certain day—say, five weeks ago?'

Morrissey watched the sergeant put on his most disarming smile; the one Janet Yarby had been heard to say Casanova would have envied. This time, Morrissey hoped, it was strictly in the line of duty. Appleby's secretary absorbed it.

'Depends,' she said, and led them into the sales manager's office. With the window closed, the stale cigarette smell was stronger. Behind the desk, to the left of the window, a yearly planner was stretched on the wall. She peered at it. 'Five weeks ago today he was in the office. There, look, he always writes the word *in* when he's in.'

Morrissey squinted at Barrett. The sergeant ran his finger along until it stopped on the fifteenth of March.

'This has a D,' he said. 'What would that mean?'

'D for Durham. He had a sales conference. That means he was out all day.'

Morrissey's eyes had found the fifth of February. He said, 'And what does a straight line mean?'

'It means he took a day off.'

Barrett asked confidentially, 'Good boss, is he? Have you worked for him a long time?'

'Three years, and he's all right, yes.'

'You must have known Diane Anderson, then,' Morrissey said. 'She did some temping here about eighteen months ago. Would she have done any work for Mr Appleby?'

With a shake of her head Karen Breen said quickly, 'No, she was just doing invoice typing, that's all.' She folded her arms into V-shapes, gripping her shoulders. 'It's getting really scary. I'm glad I live with my boyfriend; I wouldn't like to go out on my own.'

But many women had to; chose to. Like Katie. Margaret too, come to that. He closed his mind to the unthinkable, and said, 'Did you talk to her much?'

'Not really; just hello and that sort of thing in the canteen. You asked all that before when it...when she died. Not you personally. Someone else came.'

'I know,' said Morrissey, 'but sometimes things get forgotten, small bits that might be useful. It doesn't hurt to ask again. For instance, why did she leave? Did anyone ask that?'

'I don't remember. I suppose we just didn't need a temp any longer.'

Barrett said casually, 'Do you know anyone called Rob?'

She laughed at that, a bit shakily, but glad to change the subject. 'Who doesn't? There's Robby Clamp in packing, and Robert Hall in wages, and then there's my Rob.'

'Your Rob,' said Morrissey. 'Who would that be?'

'Rob Wells. My boyfriend.'

'And what's his job?' Barrett asked, eager now, the smile gone. 'Does he work here?'

She shook her head and her own smile widened, as if she were sharing a joke with them. 'He's a policeman,' she said. 'Like you.'

'QUITE SURPRISING how many Roberts and Robs are turning up,' Morrissey said complacently as they drove away from Crowther's.

Barrett stared at the road. The chief liked to rub things in. What did it matter how many Robs there were when they'd just established the fact that Appleby hadn't been in his office when the three girls died. Of course, Morrissey being Morrissey, he'd say that was circumstantial too, but to Barrett's mind that's what they should be following up. Instead of which they were going to dig through every Rob, Robert and Robin on the payroll. And not only at Crowther's, but at every other place the dead girls had worked.

Morrissey said, 'Should be a full day's work for you tomorrow; I'll arrange for Smythe and Copeland to give you a hand.'

In tight, polite formality, Barrett asked, 'What about Appleby, sir?'

'I'll get round to him,' Morrissey said. 'You needn't worry about that.' But it would be gently, softly, so as not to alarm, the chief inspector thought. Far better that than a hammer.

Barrett said. 'I still don't understand why no one found out until now that Diane Anderson had asked to be moved. Questions have been asked at both Crowther's and Redfearn's before.'

'But not the right one,' said Morrissey. 'And that being so, you'd better make sure that when you come back tomorrow it's top of your list.'

But it wouldn't be there alone, thought Barrett. He had a question of his own to ask. About Appleby.

SEVEN

SMYTHE AND LATIMER were still in the canteen. Latimer's face looked even paler and there was a plate of almost untouched food on the table before him. Morrissey sat himself on an empty chair.

Smythe said politely, 'Coffee, sir?'

'Tea.' The chief inspector grimaced. 'And I don't want paint-stripper.'

Smythe grinned, then wondered on his way to the counter if stomach problems were an inevitable consequence of the job.

Left alone with Latimer, Morrissey asked, 'How did you come? Car? Train?'

'Train. The van's in the station yard. I didn't feel up to the motorway; I've no great love for the M62 at the best of times.'

'Sensible; not easy to keep your mind on driving when you're facing something unpleasant. There'll be other things too, after the inquest.'

Latimer knew what he meant. 'I'll see to the funeral. I don't want her left here, though. I'll take her back home.'

If eyes could be haunted by things not done, then Latimer's were, Morrissey thought. He said, 'Whatever you want. There'll be compensation to come

eventually, not much, but it will help with expenses.'
It sounded clumsy, and he despised its having to be
said.

'Money?' Colour rushed into the pale face and out
again. 'What the hell has money to do with it?'

'Nothing,' Morrissey apologised. 'It's just one of
the things I'm supposed to tell you. There's something else. You know about the page three photograph? Gail told you?'

Latimer nodded. 'Is that why the bastard ...?'

'No. We've nothing to suggest that, but if the Press,
certain sections of it, find out you're her brother,
they'll be on the doorstep. We shan't release that information here; be careful who you talk to back
home. And warn your wife.'

'When you find him ...' Latimer said intensely.

'I'll make very sure you're told, well before you
read it in the papers,' Morrissey promised.

Smythe brought tea the colour of mahogany.
'Thanks,' the chief inspector said wearily, and took a
gulp at it. The taste was of pure tannin. He pushed the
half-pint mug away.

LORRAINE DIDN'T HEAR about the murder until she
went in to work, and found the whole place was
buzzing with it.

'*I* can't see how you missed hearing about it before
now!' Joni Thompson threw one of her smart looks.
'Must be love. I'd say it'll be a good thing when that
wedding's over and your brain starts working again.'

Lorraine, who had spent the night at Malcolm's and had had to run for the bus without breakfast, felt her stomach flop, and let the insult pass. 'Oh, my God, I think I heard it!' she said. 'It must have been her, poor silly cow, screaming when me and Mal were in that bus shelter on Mortimer Road. Mal said it was larking about. Oh, my God, and I've got her umbrella! Oh, my God!' She flopped on to the chair in front of her sewing-machine and went cold.

'Well, I wouldn't shout about it then, if I was you,' Joni said, 'since your Mal's got a right randy reputation. That's three now, and any scapegoat's better than none.'

'They wouldn't!' Lorraine said.

'Risk it, then,' said Joni. 'They have visiting days.' She went to sit behind her own machine.

Lorraine tried to thread cotton, stabbing at the needle's eye. The umbrella was at Malcolm's. It would have his fingerprints all over it.

She fretted until finishing time came and she could run for the bus and wait for him coming home.

BARRETT HAD almost finished organising the next day's round of questioning, and Morrissey was on the point of leaving. It was almost six, and he had a fancy to catch Appleby on his home territory. That way he might pick up signs of tension, something to suggest that all wasn't well between husband and wife. The police psychiatrist had raised that point. He hadn't dismissed the idea of Appleby as an attacker, merely raised questions that needed to be asked.

By Morrissey... somehow.

The internal telephone rang and gave a temporary reprieve. The desk sergeant's voice said, 'There's a young couple here claiming information about the Latimer murder: Malcolm Livesey and Lorraine Shaw. Seems they were near the common. Do you want me to send them up?'

'Please, Bill.'

Barrett looked up from his pile of forms. 'Anything?'

'Hopeful.'

The chief inspector resettled his buttocks, and heard the chair groan. He ignored the warning.

When the door opened, Lorraine came in first, looking terrified. Malcolm Livesey held her hand firmly. Morrissey saw the rolled-up plastic carrier bag in his other hand and wondered what was in it.

He tried to instil reassurance into his voice. 'I shan't bite. Sit down and tell me what the worry is.' The couple moved forward. Protective again, the man edged his chair closer to the girl's.

Her long bright red earrings swung. Round eyed, she said, 'We were there. Mal thought...I thought...'

Malcolm said, 'Somebody larking. That's what it sounded like. I was going to have a look.' He was defensive.

Lorraine cut in, 'It was me that stopped him. I thought he might get hurt.'

'Why should he? Not if it was just larking,' Morrissey said reasonably. 'What time was this?'

'Two-ish.'

'Quarter to,' Malcolm corrected. 'The bus passed us just before it started raining.' He looked at Morrissey. 'It was the twenty-five to. If I hadn't thought the rain would hold off a bit longer, we'd have caught it.'

'I wish we had,' said Lorraine.

Morrissey said, 'Just what was it you heard or saw?'

'Heard,' Lorraine asserted. 'We'd both got a half-day off, you see...to go shopping. We're getting married, and Mal was taking me to choose a wedding ring. Then, when it rained, we went into the bus shelter to wait a bit, and I was talking to Mal about bridesmaids' dresses and...'

Morrissey blinked, and Malcolm cut in quickly. 'It was a scream.' He reached for Lorraine's hand. 'We couldn't see anything, and I said it must be somebody larking about. I mean, you don't expect... Well, not in broad daylight. Only then there was the umbrella.' He leaned forward and set the plastic bag on Morrissey's desk. 'It was open. Bowling down the hill by itself. We watched it for a bit to see if anybody came after it.'

'But you didn't see anybody?'

'No.'

'And then what happened?' Morrissey watched the two pairs of eyes meet. 'It could be very helpful,' he encouraged.

'I went and got the umbrella,' Malcolm admitted.

Lorraine said, 'We were going to hand it in. We weren't going to keep it; only, when no one came for it, it seemed a shame. I mean, it kept us dry when we made a dash for it. For town. The other bus stop.'

'We caught the quarter-past two on the main road,' Malcolm said. 'When I went for the umbrella, I was going to go up the hill and have a look, but...'

'I stopped him,' Lorraine said again, her voice higher. 'He would have gone if I hadn't. I wish, I wish...' She shut up, not knowing exactly what she wished. To know if it would have made a difference, probably, but afraid of Morrissey saying yes.

The chief inspector unrolled the carrier bag but didn't touch its contents. 'You've both handled this?'

'Yes.'

'Anybody else?'

'No.'

'You won't mind giving us your fingerprints? We'll need them to compare with whatever we find on it. They'll be destroyed afterwards.'

'Now?' Malcolm said.

'Before you leave. Which way did you walk to the common?'

'Down Manorfield Lane from Pearce's Cottages—Lorraine's mam and dad live there. Then past the top of the common and down Mortimer Road, the bus went past, and two or three cars.'

'Nobody parked?'

'I don't think so.'

'There was a police car,' Lorraine said. 'On Manorfield Lane, just before it turns on to Mortimer Road. It looked as if he was writing.'

'The driver? By himself, was he?'

Lorraine nodded.

Malcolm said. 'Nobody else, though.'

Lorraine came back. 'Yes, there was. There was Rington's Tea.'

'What?'

'At them houses on the crescent.'

'Oh yeah, I'd forgotten him. Nobody walking, though.'

'No,' she agreed. 'Nobody walking.'

'And no one got off the bus?'

'No. There was a whole lot got on, though.'

And Gail Latimer had been on her way to catch a bus. Not that one, though. 'What time was the next one due?' Morrissey asked.

'Five to.'

'Why didn't you catch that instead of going to the main road?'

Lorraine looked at him pityingly, condescendingly. 'It's twenty pence more from there,' she said. 'We don't waste money; not when we've got feet.'

EIGHT

THE FIRST GIRL had been a mistake, but by the time he saw her face, it was too late because she'd seen his, too, and could have pointed him out. Women fouled up everything. Silly bitch! Straddling her, tightening the ligature round her neck he'd had an erection.

When he got home he was sick. Foul, rancid sick.

After it wore off there was elation. He couldn't remember a time when there'd been such an overwhelming sense of his own existence. He'd felt godlike. The power of life and death in his hands.

And the next day...seeing the police crawling round on their hands and knees, and knowing he'd got away with it because there was no connection between the girl and him. No provable connection, that was the point.

The sense of elation came back, and without thinking where he was, he laughed out loud. There was a child in front of him, orange-mouthed from the ice-lolly in her hand, her eyes round and staring as he laughed. He forced himself to wink and smile, watching as she skipped away. The up and down movement sent the short pink skirt bouncing above her white knickers and he let his mind dwell on that until she was out of sight, retaining the after-image until his mind tired of it and slithered on to the second killing.

It hadn't been some silly bitch wearing the same colour coat that time.

He'd let Diane see him, deliberately stood in front of her wanting to be recognised, seen her working out what he wanted and known the thought in her mind was rape. The erection that came when his hands were tight on the twine around her throat had climaxed violently, and he squatted over her for some minutes after it had subsided, feeling confident and secure. He'd wondered when it was over, as he wondered now, if in fact that last second she had known why she was going to die. It annoyed him now, as it had disappointed him then, that her face had shown surprise, not fear.

As if she didn't think he had it in him.

On the television news next day there had been pictures of the police combing the ground, looking like blue-bottles on a butcher's slab; scrabbling around, picking up useless bits of rubbish, shoving them into plastic bags.

Clueless!

Across the road the child with white knickers was back and staring at him, eyes wide like the Price girl's had been the Sunday he followed her home along the towpath. She'd worn white knickers, too. He'd been twelve then, twice her age, twice her size, and he'd put his hand up her skirt. She'd kicked and wriggled, and threatened to tell. Rubbish, like Diane. He'd shoved her backwards to shut her up, and her mouth had been a wide O as she went into the canal. For a minute he'd worried she might be able to swim, but she hadn't, she'd drowned like the kittens his mother made him dump in the water-butt years before.

Killing was easy; he could do it when he wanted and not get caught. He'd done it again when the thunderstorm brewed up over the common, and he'd seen the girl in the shiny black raincoat alone, and scurrying like a beetle. She'd been a bonus. He remembered the spinning umbrella and stretched his shoulders, arms flexed.

When the dark blue car turned the corner at the bottom of the common and he recognised Morrissey behind the wheel, he smiled and moved away.

NINE

As HE TURNED INTO Mortimer Road, Morrissey recognised Appleby and thought that the recognition had been mutual. He stopped outside the house with its green and white For Sale sign and got out.

Caught mid-way between gate and front door, Appleby hesitated. 'Chief Inspector. Were you wanting to see me?'

'If it isn't inconvenient.'

Or, come to that, even if it was, but it paid not to point such things out. Yet.

Appleby's wife must have been watching from the window because she opened the door before her husband reached it, looking past him to Morrissey. She gave an impression of nervousness, but then so did a lot of people when they found themselves involved with the police. He reminded himself that an anxious wife didn't necessarily imply a knowledge of guilt.

'Chief Inspector. I thought you'd already spoken to Brian?'

'I have, Mrs Appleby, but something else has come up that I hope he can help me with. I'll try not to disturb the evening too much for you.'

'It's all right, Gwen. I'm not about to be arrested!' Morrissey saw the man's arm go round his wife's shoulders; it seemed a natural gesture. No tension there. Or, at least, not on the surface. The chief inspector reminded himself that the middle classes were consummate masters of the police cover-up where marital problems were concerned. He stepped in to the hall.

Appleby had a pack of ice-cream in his hand; his wife took it from him. 'I'll put this in the freezer,' she said, and moved away.

'We'll talk in here.'

Morrissey followed Appleby into a chintzy, calm room. There was a profusion of photographs, mostly of the same two children in different moods and various ages. Growing up, slipping away. The thought was unwanted and brought with it a feeling of regret. Katie would soon be gone, too. He moved to look at the bookshelves.

'A hotch-potch,' Appleby told him from behind. 'Some mine, some Gwen's, some left over from the children. They're not in any kind of order, except by author.'

What am I being told? Morrissey wondered. That looking at the mass of titles wouldn't give him a psychological profile?

'And the Highsmiths?' he said. 'Yours?'

Appleby hesitated. 'Shared,' he said. 'A common enjoyment. You've read some of them yourself?'

'Some,' Morrissey admitted. 'I find Ripley a hard character to come to terms with. Professional prejudice, I suppose.'

He got a gleam of understanding. 'Like the fish that got away?'

'Perhaps.' Morrissey turned. 'A girl called Diane Anderson worked at Crowther's for a while last summer, a temp from Redfearn's. Did you have any contact with her?'

'There's been a flow of temporary workers over the past year. Too many for me to remember even if I normally came into contact with all of them—which I don't. I'm sorry, Chief Inspector, but if you had asked my secretary when you were there this afternoon, she would have told you that she allocates excess work herself.'

And that made it clear Appleby knew what questions had been asked in his absence; and knew what Morrissey had come to ask now.

'I don't really understand why you've come here, Chief Inspector. Not when I've heard that all Crowther's staff are to be questioned again tomorrow.'

'The third murder was almost opposite your house. If you were home for lunch that day, you might have noticed a parked car.'

'But I wasn't home, and my wife has already said she saw and heard nothing.'

Morrissey walked to the window and looked towards the common. The copse was in plain view at the top of the scrubby rise of land, but nothing could be seen past the first straggle of bushes. He said conversationally, 'What were you doing between twelve

o'clock and two o'clock yesterday?' and turned agate eyes on Appleby. An edge came to his voice. 'I'll
need to know exactly.'

'I don't think I'm obliged . . .'

'In a murder investigation, everyone is obliged.
Especially someone who can be proved to have had
contact with two of the victims. Diane Anderson
asked to be moved from Crowther's because of sexual harassment. Gail Latimer, we know, came here to
your house and you were alone with her.'

'Dear God! Do you think I'm some kind of mon-
ster? I didn't know Diane Anderson—I never met the
girl—and the other was plain coincidence.'

'Then there's no reason for you not to tell me exactly what you did between twelve and two yesterday.'

Appleby slumped into one of the easy chairs. 'Sit
down, for heaven's sake,' he said, 'and let me get used
to the idea of being a murder suspect.'

Morrissey sat on the settee. He prompted, 'Your
secretary went for lunch at twelve-thirty.'

'Yes, I know; she went early. I went out soon afterwards; about a quarter to one, I should think. I
walked to the Crown and had a bar meal. It must have
been about half-past one when I left. Then I walked
into town. I wanted to look for something special for
Gwen; it's our wedding anniversary next week.'

Morrissey winced. A good and faithful husband?
'And you arrived back at Crowther's when?'

'Just before two-thirty.'

'A long lunch-hour.'

'Crowther's gain more time than they lose, Chief Inspector.'

'Did you have a drink at the Crown?'

'A half of real ale.'

'And would they remember you if I had to ask?'

'I shared a table with Bob Crane, a fellow Rotarian.'

'What about afterwards, when you went shopping in Malminster? Did you meet anyone there who would remember it?'

'No,' said Appleby. 'Not a bloody soul.' He looked at Morrissey. 'So there you have it; no alibi.'

'The fifth of February and the fifteenth of March.'

'You want me to remember them?'

'If you could.' He didn't doubt that Karen Breen would already have told Appleby the dates they were interested in.

'The February date, Gwen was ill, I took a day off to look after her, and I can't tell you what I did with every minute of my time. On the fifteenth of March I was at a sales conference in Durham, and yes, I was late getting home; very late. The car got a flat, and a hub-nut jammed.'

There was a sound outside the door. Appleby leaned forward and said urgently, 'Don't say anything in front of Gwen. She soon gets depressed.'

The police psychiatrist had said, 'If you can't bring yourself to ask the big question, look for a depressed wife. Problems on the top floor often stem from trouble in the basement.'

Gwen Appleby came in with a tray. She said brightly, 'I thought it would be nice if we all had a cup of coffee.' The smile she gave Morrissey had something of wistfulness in it. 'I wish you were here under pleasanter circumstances, Chief Inspector. Fewer people call now that the children are gone. No more parties, no more pop music to loosen the roof tiles.'

'A big house,' Morrissey said, 'for just two people.'

'Too big and too empty. That's why we want to sell.' She frowned at her husband. 'Perhaps we should change agents?'

'Give them time. Property isn't easy to move just now. They're doing their best.'

'The trouble is, of course, after yesterday's dreadful event, people will be put off.' She gave Morrissey another smile and a cup of coffee. 'Although I do seem to remember that when the Black Panther's house was sold in Bradford, there was a queue of people wanting to buy.'

Morrissey swallowed and half choked. Eyes watering, he wondered if Appleby's wife had any idea of the possible significance of what she had just said.

Appleby certainly did; he seemed frozen in his chair.

Her smile fading, his wife blinked from one man to the other. 'I've startled you both,' she said, 'but it's quite true. I remember reading about it in the paper.'

TEN

MORRISSEY HAD intended going straight home when he left Appleby, but instead he went back to the office, telling himself the paperwork was urgent enough to warrant doing then and there, but knowing all the time the real reason was something else altogether.

At nine-thirty he gave up the pretence and went home, letting the car remember its way up Middlebrook Road and round the roundabout at the top. There was a street light out half-way along Forest Drive, just before the solidly built semi where Margaret would be waiting. The patch of blackness irritated him and he switched on his headlights, seeing a swirl of dried leaves and dust as the Peebles' black and white cat leapt for the top of the wooden fence and into next door's garden. He turned into his drive, gladdened by the gleam of light through closed curtains.

Margaret was in her favourite chair, sewing up a mohair jumper she'd been knitting for Katie, the mass of it on her lap, fluffy, like a bright purple kitten. She looked at her husband without saying anything, seeing tiredness, but refusing for once to be moved by it.

He said, 'Pretty.'

She held the knitting at arm's length, head on one side, critical of her own work. 'Not bad, I suppose; she likes purple.'

'It would suit you.'

Margaret glanced at him, silent again. Long, silky mohair suggested dressing up. Going out. Not the sort of thing to wear at committee meetings or the supermarket. Frustration at the rarity of being half a couple simmered, and she lowered her head, beginning to sew again.

'There's a casserole in the oven. It just needs putting on a plate. I'll make some coffee in a minute when I've finished this.'

He rested a tentative hand on her shoulder and felt stiff resistance. She didn't look up. He went into the kitchen and burned his thumb taking the casserole from the oven, sucking at it and cursing as though it had been deliberately planned to cause him pain. Only when he was eating and his stomach began to settle comfortably did he admit it wasn't his wife's fault.

Margaret came in and began making coffee before he had finished eating. She said, 'I wish Katie had a steady boyfriend, someone who'd walk her home. Thank God we're moving into summer and the daylight is lengthening.'

Last week Katie had talked about driving lessons, about having a car of her own to take her backwards and forwards to college. He'd agreed to the lessons but not the car. She must share the small Fiat with her mother, he'd said, which meant she would rarely get to drive it at all. If she went out, it was usually straight from college without coming home first.

Katie had pointed that out. Morrissey had tartly said that his job was to protect banks, not rob them.

Since then, another girl had died, and Margaret's words were a reminder that his daughter was vulnerable, too. He forbore to point out that darkness wasn't necessarily a danger, that Gail Latimer had died in mid-afternoon.

'I'll talk to her,' he said.

'When?' his wife asked sharply, knowing that now this new investigation had begun, the chances of husband and daughter meeting long enough to talk were remote.

For the first time, he realised that the house was silent. 'When she comes in?' he suggested.

'Then it won't be tonight; the college disco goes on until two, and she's crashing with a friend.' She set a coffee mug near him and stood, sipping from her own. 'And I can't damn well insist she rings me when she gets there because it would embarrass her.'

Morrissey said. 'The chances...'

Margaret interrupted. 'I know. It's something I've been telling myself every half-hour.'

And Mike was on a field trip with the school. Which meant that Margaret had been sitting alone in the house while he'd been inventing reasons not to be there. Guilt prodded with sharp spurs. 'The book...'

he said awkwardly. 'The Dylan Thomas. I haven't said thank you yet.'

She shrugged. 'It was just a book. And the roses are nice.'

He cringed inwardly. *Nice*. And they were already falling; he'd noticed two petals lying near the vase. Abruptly he turned his thoughts back to Katie. 'Has she sorted out a driving school yet, decided who she wants?'

'Katie,' said Margaret shortly, at odds now with both husband and daughter, 'is being awkward. She says what's the point in learning to drive if she hasn't a car. She says it very reasonably, and I feel like shaking her.' Sitting down at last, she put her elbows on the table, the mug still cupped in her hands. 'By our own deeds we are undone,' she said softly. 'I teach her to be logical and she uses it against me. I can't win.'

But she already has, he thought, and Katie too. He pushed his empty plate away. 'She'd have to work Saturdays to pay for petrol,' he said. 'Tell her that.'

Margaret's eyes glowed; she set the mug down and reached out to his hand. 'John...'

'Yes, I know I'm a soft touch,' he agreed, and thought it would be cheap at the price if it set things right between them again.

What he didn't say was that the most dangerous time, for Katie and every other young woman in Malminster, was now, and that driving lessons couldn't act like a talisman to ward off evil.

BARRETT MADE an early start at Crowther's. When the first workers arrived just before eight-thirty, he and the two detective constables were ensconced in a hastily cleared office on the first floor. Thoughtfully someone had provided a kettle; it sat on a tin tray near the window on top of a dumpy filing cabinet, and rubbed shoulders with a jar of own-brand instant coffee and a dozen tea-bags in a chipped cup.

'What're we supposed to drink it out of?' said Smythe.

'Canteen's downstairs,' Copeland offered. 'I'll nip and get some cups before we start.'

'Clairvoyant detection?' asked Barrett.

'I was here last time. We didn't get a kettle then.'

'You didn't get the right questions asked, either. If you had, I'd be doing something more interesting now.'

Barrett was still not pleased at his day's task. The chief would have said that most detective work was ninety-nine parts solid sifting, but Barrett wanted more chance to go for the one per cent hunch.

'You should have told us we were looking for somebody called Rob,' Smythe pointed out. 'Then we would've, wouldn't we?'

Let Barrett get round that, he thought, resenting the cockiness that suggested the DS was doing everyone a favour by just being there.

'If you'd found out that Diane Anderson left because she was being sexually harassed, you might have discovered it for yourself,' Barrett said shorttemperedly. And, to Copeland, 'See if you can grab a few biscuits while you're down there.'

As Copeland went out, he surreptitiously eyed Barrett's straining grey pin-stripe waistcoat. The DS fancied himself; birds fell off trees for him. The DC reflected on the injustice of life. Then he remembered a bit of psychology: food was a comfort symbol. His mind made the connection, and he began to whistle cheerfully.

THE SECOND ROUND of questioning at Crowther's brought nothing new, and the casual questions Barrett slipped in about Appleby's attitude to women employees gave him no joy at all. The sales manager was apparently a walking example of rectitude. As to Diane Anderson's complaint of sexual harassment, the carefully phrased questions got nothing except blank looks. Only one pale light gleamed.

A cheerful wages clerk, with freckles spilling over her face, said, 'It's Lucy Foster you want to talk to. She was the one who got really friendly with Diane while she was here. Last time your lot came she was that upset she could do nothing but cry, but if there was anything going on it'd be her Diane told.' She gave Barrett a wide smile. 'Trouble is, you'll have to wait a bit. She's in Acapulco on her honeymoon.'

Barrett scowled at Lucy Foster's bad timing. 'When does she get back?'

'Another ten days yet.' She smiled again. 'You'll have to come back, won't you? Home from home before long.'

Unless we've nailed Appleby by then, Barrett thought as he watched her leave, her short skirt swinging jauntily.

'I think that one fancies you,' Copeland said from the depths of his new knowledge. Barrett's hand went to his tie. Something else that might be worth following up.

It was almost twelve when they were through. As they were packing their things away, the personnel manager stuck his head in. 'The canteen can cope if you fancy eating there.'

'I think I fancy a pub meal,' Barrett said, 'but thanks all the same. Any idea which is the best and nearest?'

'Oh, the Crown, no doubt about it. I often eat there. Go out the back entrance, across the yard, over the access road and through the ginnel. It brings you out in Burton Street, turn right, cross over the road, down Carter Street and you're out into Queen's Road. The Crown's facing you. I recommend their steak pie.' He blinked, realising that Barrett was bristling like a terrier.

'Carter Street,' the detective-sergeant said slowly. 'Down Carter Street. Is there a newsagent there?'

'Yes, Bowlby's.' Understanding crossed his face. 'Of course—coincidence, isn't it? The first one worked there. Nice kid; she didn't deserve it.'

'No one does,' said Smythe.

'No, of course not. I meant ...'

As he groped for words, Barrett said crisply, 'I suppose a lot of people here would call in to buy a paper on their way to the Crown?'

'Well, yes, that's right. Handy. I do myself.'

'And I know Mr Appleby buys one sometimes; he told me so himself. Would he get it there?'

'Oh yes, usually. We walk down together quite often ... Friendly shop.'

Having found a scent, Barrett was satisfied. He'd closed the circle. To hell with its being circumstantial; Appleby was in the middle of the picture, and not even Morrissey could avoid admitting it now.

ELEVEN

MORRISSEY HAD started the day cheerfully, taking the steps to his office two at a time as usual. Each forward thrust of movement sent his arms leaping from the cuffs of his shirt, and the center vent of his jacket rucked and gaped. He knew these things happened but seldom thought about it consciously, and when he did, it was with amusement and a wry condemnation of a tailoring trade that made little allowance for long limbs.

Margaret occasionally let exasperation show by demanding that he have his next suit tailored, but inevitably when the time came he bought it off the peg, and in the sales. It was a remembrance that brought with it the realisation that for the first time in three days he had thought of his wife without guilt.

The cheerful mood had lasted until he got Osgodby's summons. He had gone upstairs sensing he wouldn't like the reason for it.

Unease showed in the chief superintendent's tapping fingers. 'Glad I caught you, John. You'll have seen the papers, like everybody else, including the CC? He's been on my back already, asking stroppy questions and making noises about Regional Crime Squad.'

'They're not a magic elite,' said Morrissey sourly. 'I doubt they'd do better.'

'No, no, that's right. I said as much myself, but you know how things go, it's on the cards.' Osgodby looked genuinely put out. His lips pursed, then thinned. 'There's another thing.' The fingers tapped harder. 'The CC wants you available for a press conference at ten-thirty.'

Morrissey leaned back in the chair. 'It's time-wasting.' The protest was as useless as his presence at the conference would be. The CC would talk about progress and important new leads. Osgodby would back him up, and he, Morrissey, wouldn't be asked to say anything at all, except perhaps to agree they were following positive lines of enquiry.

But, when it came, the question he was asked wasn't about lines of enquiry, it was about the mind of the man they were looking for. Claiming to be repeating the opinion of a psychiatrist, a reporter suggested that the absence of any form of sexual assault on the victims showed that the killer was afraid of women. Didn't that in its turn show a cowardly nature in the man Morrissey was looking for?

Morrissey fenced politely, replying that he had no reason to disagree with a consultant psychiatrist's professional opinion. He thought it was a safe answer.

When the meeting ended at eleven, he was chafing to be away. Without Osgodby's intervention, he would have been knocking on the door of Gail Latimer's foster parents more than an hour ago. Now, he'd be lucky to find anyone in. His stomach rumbled and stabbed.

It was an annoyance that the dead girl seemed to have had no real social life; she belonged to no clubs, attended no night classes. According to Susan Reed, except at the times she was working, Gail had been a home bird without any men friends.

But that couldn't be entirely true because there was Rob. Or was there? Would a lonely girl invent a boyfriend?

That led on to another question. Why would a girl as attractive as Gail be lonely? It was illogical, and the flaw bothered him.

He took the questions with him to the box-shaped semi-detached house where her foster parents lived, expecting, at best, to find Mrs Nolan and surprised to find them both.

Nolan, gauntly angular, with a flick of lank black hair drooping down his forehead, was dismissive. The Adam's apple in his long neck moved when he laughed.

'If you've got Gail down as backward at coming forward, then you're wrong. More of a raver than anything.' He gave Morrissey a broad wink as if they shared some masculine joke. 'Well, you must know, you'll have had medical reports. Not a virgin, was she, eh? Not for a long time.'

The chief inspector eyed him with antipathy, seeing an eager carrion-picker in the sharp features.

Nolan would like to hear all the details; would lap them up and come for more. 'Then when she lived here you knew she had boyfriends,' Morrissey said. 'I expect she brought them home?'

'Oh no, not here. She wouldn't, would she, in case we told her social worker.'

'What difference would that have made?' asked Morrissey, who had never yet met a censorious social worker. 'At most, she would have had some counselling, I would have thought that's what fostering was all about: doing what was best for the child. Knowing what kind of trouble they were getting in; who their friends were.'

'That's what we tried to do, isn't it, Jeannie?'

Jeannie, who had a different kind of thinness from her husband, agreed, her head nodding in limp acquiescence. She had stayed on the far side of the room, framed in the kitchen doorway, mixing something in a bowl. Morrissey sought for a word to describe her, and the only word that came was bloodless.

'But you've already told me she wasn't allowed to bring friends home, so how could you know what she was up to? How long have you been fostering?'

'Eight or nine years, since Sharon grew up.'

'Sharon is your own daughter?'

Jeannie stopped mixing whatever it was and looked at him. Her husband said, 'Yes, but you know what teenagers are like, these days. Moved away as soon as she left school. Jeannie still sees her, though, don't you, love?'

Another nod.

'But not you?'

'Sharon was a mother's girl.'

Was, not *is*. Nolan had dismissed his daughter from his life. 'I'd like her address,' said Morrissey.

'What for? She didn't know Gail.'

'Nevertheless.'

'Nevertheless you've got to have a reason to ask, and I don't think you've got one. No, I'm sorry, I'll not give it to you.'

'Fostering a child at the moment, are you, Mr Nolan?' the chief inspector asked gently. 'I expect it's very rewarding.'

'If you mean money, no, it's not. A lot less than we spend, I should think. Jeannie sees to that.' He looked at his wife. 'Less, is it, love?'

Did the woman do nothing but nod?

Morrissey said encouragingly, 'I expect you must enjoy being a foster mother, knowing there'll always be a child around. Growing up, sharing things.'

She stared at the chief inspector with faint pink coming into her cheeks, then without a word she turned her back on him and went into the kitchen.

Morrissey blinked and turned hard eyes on the bony man, who looked suddenly uncomfortable. The sitting-room was almost fanatically tidy and dust free. There were no playthings, no comics or children's books, or crayons carelessly left for later use.

'Who did you say you were fostering now?'

'Another girl. Tracy Lambton. She's at school.'

'Fisher's?'

'Eskdale Road.'

'Middle school. Only young, then?'

'Ten. She's been living with us a year.'

Morrissey made a note, and said mildly, 'Ever thought of moving back to Leeds?'

That startled Nolan. He was suddenly wary. 'Leeds? Back to Leeds? Is that supposed to mean something?'

'You lived there in nineteen seventy-two, before you came here. Burley, wasn't it?'

Nolan said, 'I thought you'd come about Gail. I haven't seen her since she left, and that's two years now. Not to talk to, anyway. I've seen her in the street once or twice, and I saw her picture in the *Sun*, and that's all.'

'And you've no idea who any of her boyfriends were, not even while she lived here?'

'She never told me.'

Morrissey moved across the room to the kitchen. Mrs Nolan looked around, seeing Morrissey's body blocking the doorway.

'She didn't tell me any names, either, so it's no good asking.' Her voice now he heard it was almost sing-song, like a recitation.

Morrissey looked from one to the other. 'Aren't you bothered what they get up to when they're out of the house?' He looked at Nolan. 'Where do you work?'

'Middleton's Soft Drinks. I'm night-foreman. I'd have been in bed by now if you hadn't come.'

Morrissey moved away from the kitchen, back into the sitting-room.

'Middleton's. Up on the industrial estate near Crowther's Biscuits. I remember noticing they'd moved up there.' He fixed Nolan stonily. 'There've been three murders, and a girl named Diane Anderson was the second. She worked at Crowther's. I suppose you might even have seen her? Casually; when you were at work, coming or going. Met her, even? Spoken? Funny coincidence.'

Nolan's throat became over-active. 'That's all it would have been, just blind coincidence. There's a stream of girls and women working up there; I'm not going to remember any one in particular, am I? Not unless I had reason to.'

'Somebody does,' Morrissey reminded him. 'Somebody remembers, because they killed them. That's something to think about, isn't it, Mr Nolan? Carefully, if I were you.'

The chief inspector strode away, out of the house and down the path to his car.

The Nolans' foster child wasn't Morrissey's concern. Officially. But first Gail's brother and then knowledge of the Leeds business had started a worry. And now that he had met the Nolans for himself, the worry had been magnified. Even so, if it had been any

school other than Eskdale he would probably have let
it ride for the time being. But Matthew Haines was
the headmaster, and Matt was a personal friend.

He found him alone in the staff-room, sitting forward on a chair with the television turned on. His
posture gave him the guilty look of a truant rather
than a teacher, and when he saw Morrissey he raised
a hand and shook his head. 'Better listen,' he said.
'This bit's about you.'

Morrissey closed the door and sat down, watching
the mid-day news bulletin. On a screen behind the
news-reader was a freeze shot of that morning's conference, with light reflecting from the shiny pink skin
under Osgodby's thinning sandy hair.

'*The Chief Constable stated that progress is now
being made on several lines of enquiry*.' A solemn
look. '*The investigative officer, Chief Inspector John
Morrissey, backed up the opinion given by a psychiatrist that the wanted man could be described as a
coward*.' A censorious look. '*Perhaps it would have
been better said—a dangerous coward. The advice to
women is to avoid isolated areas, and to have a male
escort whenever possible*.'

Morrissey rolled his eyes heavenward as the bulletin ended. Haines snapped off the set, saying, 'I always watch the local news at this time when I get the
chance. Have done since we got caught out by the bus
strike.'

'I hope it's usually more accurate than that.'

'Misquote?'

'Out of context, too. Can we have five minutes in your office?'

'As long as you like, or at least…' he looked at his watch, 'until half-past, then I've got playground duty. Share it with me, if you like. I'll introduce you to some future crime statistics.'

'Ignorance is bliss,' Morrissey said. As they crossed the corridor he began to talk about Tracy Lambton and the Nolans, knowing that all he could offer Matt was subjective feelings; any mention of the old Leeds incident had to be avoided.

But the headmaster already had worries of his own. 'Tracy's certainly been getting more withdrawn over the last few months. I asked education welfare to visit, but the trouble is that sort of problem isn't visible; it's like dirt under a carpet.' He raised his hands. 'The hell with it, it's medicals tomorrow. I'll have a word with the MO. Let you know if anything comes of it.'

Morrissey said heavily, 'Glad if you would,' staring through the window at the deserted playground. It wasn't the first time he'd had cause to wonder if mankind had begun its long descent back to the brutes.

It was the job, of course. The people he dealt with were lawbreakers, society's rejects. It was hard to remember that the majority of people were still peaceably honest.

There'd been an oil-spill years ago, off the Lincolnshire coast; not a bad one, but unusual, then.

It had spread darkly on the beach, leaving a black tidemark. He'd watched it grow each morning, creeping a little further up the shore. The clean bit where children could still play shrank, and paddling meant getting caked in black stuff.

He had the same feeling now, that he was watching a rising soil-mark, and was impotent to stop it.

TWELVE

Barrett was in the office, leaning on his arms over the desk, looking at a map. The chief inspector's eyebrows went up.

'Finished already?' He peered over the sergeant's shoulder and saw it was the Malminster street map.

'It's time we had a new one. This doesn't show the industrial estate,' Barrett said, busily drawing in the access roads and the sprawling estate boundary. 'It's probably nothing like, but it'll do. Crowther's are here in this corner with an access road right behind.' He squinted up at Morrissey. 'We went in the front way, but all the loading goes on at the back. The gates are here.' He scribbled again. 'I asked which pub they went to if they didn't fancy the canteen, and it turned out to be the Crown in Queen Street. A fair distance.'

Morrissey's eyes travelled back down the access road and through the interlacing streets. 'Too far if you're on foot and only an hour to spare. Where's the short cut?'

'Here.' Barrett sketched again. 'This access road used to be Clifford Street before they pulled all the houses down, and there's a ginnel nearly opposite the back gates.'

Morrissey sat his finger on it. 'Comes out in Burton Street . . .'

'And if you turn right and cross the road, you go down Carter Street to Queen Street, and Bowlby's newsagents are half-way along.' He beamed at the chief inspector. 'Most of the management eat at the Crown once or twice a week, and some of them buy a newspaper at Bowlby's to take with them.'

'Including Appleby.'

With a sigh that said it all, Barrett agreed, 'Including Appleby. And that puts him in the picture with all three.'

Morrissey's fingers moved on, found Queen Street and turned away from the Crown to where Ladbrook Road formed a T-junction, moved again in a short sweep to the private estate where the Nolans lived. There had been a newish Toyota in the drive and beyond it propped against the wall, seen but not given importance until now, a bicycle.

'He isn't the only one,' said Morrissey with a slow deliberation, and told him about Nolan.

HE'D BEEN LATE that morning, slept in and missed breakfast and had to move like the clappers to be on time. And so, when he'd seen the Pub Grub sign, he'd pulled into the car park. He wanted nothing fancy, just a ham sandwich and a glass of ale, so it didn't matter that they hadn't started serving hot lunches. The lounge-bar was nearly empty and he sat where he could get a good view of the television. He'd grown quite addicted to watching news bulletins since he'd become the main feature.

When he saw the news conference come on, he felt himself begin to smile and bit grandly into the sandwich so that his amusement shouldn't be be seen. Pillocks, the lot of them. But then the camera settled on Morrissey's face, and he heard a lot of psychiatric garbage. His hand itched to throw the ale-glass.

Coward!

He'd felt a bit of respect for Morrissey, and now there was disappointment. It was a mistake that would need to be paid for, and his mind began to work out how to exact it.

IT HAD COME DOWN to checking alibis, and even that wasn't foolproof; Morrissey knew there were many times in his life when he couldn't have proved either where he was or what he had been doing. The same must obviously apply to both Appleby and Nolan.

Appleby had still been certain about his movements when the chief inspector and Barrett had gone back to question him again, but this time he'd been edgy, standing near the window to light a cigarette, exhaling the smoke in sharp, irritable bursts. But he hadn't actually been in anybody's company at the relevant times, only between places and that meant a lot of careful checking.

Nolan, on the other hand, didn't have a clue where he had been. Or at least he claimed not to have. 'Don't keep a bloody diary, do I?' he'd protested.

'I'm a night-supervisor, not the managing director. If I was nights on, I'd have been in bed, if I was nights off, I'd either have been at home or playing darts. When Gail got killed, I was in bed, that I can tell you. I only heard it was her the day after it happened.'

'And your wife can back that up?' Barrett said quickly, his eyes moving to her.

This time Mrs Nolan was sitting down, not on the settee with her husband but on a straight-backed chair just out of his sight. Her eyes slid away from Barrett's.

Nolan screwed his neck round to look at her. 'Jeannie...?'

Staring at a point on the wall well away from any eyes, she said, 'I'd gone to Mum's, hadn't I?'

'What time, Mrs Nolan?' Morrissey watched her.

'About twelve. Gavin went up to bed just before, and I had some dinner with her. It's only once every couple of weeks,' she said defensively. 'I can't be expected to stay home all the time.'

'No, indeed. And you came home...?'

'Just before four when the kid gets back from school. I've got to be back for then so she doesn't wake Gavin up.'

She was still staring at the wall, and the chief inspector wondered whose eyes it was she didn't want to catch.

Nolan's neck moved convulsively. 'Not that day,' he said. 'Day before, wasn't it?'

'It's no use. Mum'd remember which day it was if they asked her.'

'Batty old cow! If she thought it'd get me into trouble, she would.' He wiped his hands on the legs of his pyjamas and said protestingly, 'Look, you've got me up out of bed for this and I've got to go to work tonight. I'll be dropping asleep.'

'Any callers?'

Mrs Nolan's eyes went to the mantelshelf and then slid away again. Morrissey saw the corner of a gas bill sticking out from behind the clock. If that was the day the meter had been read, Nolan didn't seem to know about it. Morrissey let him go back to bed; somehow he doubted if the man would get back to sleep.

When they drove away, Barrett still had his money on Appleby. 'There isn't any connection with Rob where Nolan's concerned,' he said, expertly cutting up a double decker bus. 'But there is with...'

'I haven't seen it written in letters of fire,' Morrissey snapped, 'that there has to be a Rob connection. And what you did then was damn near a driving offence.'

'Then why hasn't he come forward?' said Barrett, pretending he hadn't heard. 'If he and the Latimer girl were that close to setting up house, why isn't he upset and angry enough to let us know? With his name inside a heart, you can bet they did more than hold hands.'

Morrissey thought of a certain old sycamore tree and mourned lost innocence. But he couldn't provide an answer to the question.

'Drop me off, and then get back to Smythe and Copeland,' he said sourly, thinking of the manpower he needed to chase up alibis and check distances. There were boards set up in the bus station and at the stop by the common, asking passengers who had travelled on the one-fifteen bus from Manorfield to Malminster to come forward, and at each there was a uniformed officer ready to take statements.

Then there was the Rington's Tea driver. It was like a never-ending jigsaw. And the penalty for missing a piece would be another dead woman.

He said to Barrett, 'Stop in at Middleton's and see if personnel can confirm Nolan wasn't nights off on those three dates. Shouldn't take you long.'

It was nearly three, and as he dropped the chief inspector off, Barrett thought irritably that it would take too long.

Going in to the police station Morrissey was acidly aware that he hadn't eaten since early morning. He asked for sandwiches to be sent up, and while he waited started reading through the papers that had appeared on his desk.

The lengthy post-mortem report held nothing new—death had been by strangulation, and the instrument of death had been a ligature of plaited twine, the kind that gardeners use to tie up canes. The kind Morrissey himself used, that could be bought in any one of a dozen Malminster shops. Thin, green and innocent, until three strands were woven together and the ends tied to make a lethal garrotte.

Morrissey remembered Nolan, his sharp face eager.

From forensic there was too much information, enough to be frustrating. Everything movable found in the body's vicinity had been bagged for examination: sweet wrappers, cigarette ends, ice-lolly sticks, bits of grubby tissues. He sighed. And six used condoms.

But the motive for killing hadn't been sexual. Put that together with the habit of the citizens of Malminster to spread litter wherever they went, and the whole exercise came to nothing. Except that, maybe, just barely maybe, there'd be the same brand of cigarette-ends at each scene of crime with the same saliva traces, or the same sweet wrapper, or perhaps something more esoteric that would point to a new line of enquiry.

He added the papers to the fattening file, and mourned that so far there was nothing.

BARRETT RECOGNISED the short skirt, and when he looked in the rear-view mirror, he saw he hadn't been wrong. He pulled into the side of the road and waited. She didn't change her pace but moved away from the pavement edge, walking closer to the wall. Bright girl.

He wound down his window. 'Early finish, or errands?'

Her face cleared. 'Oh, it's you! Thought you might be kerb-crawling.'

'Round here, in the middle of the day?'

'You'd be surprised.' She eyed him. 'I'm going to the post office. Are you nosying or offering a lift?'

'Both.' Barrett reached to open the door, and she flopped into the passenger seat. The short skirt revealed a large expanse of thigh, more than when she was walking, and Barrett had an appreciative eye.

She said smartly, 'They're just like yours. Till you get to the top, anyway,' and laid her handbag across her lap.

Barrett pulled away from the kerb and said briefly, 'Seat-belt.'

'You haven't been to Crowther's again, have you? I mean I'm starting to get a bit worried; if we've got a nut-case working there, I'd rather know about it. I don't fancy ending up dead.'

'I haven't been there. Not this time.' He glanced at her. 'Don't you get your boyfriend to walk you home, then?'

'What makes you think I've got one? Turn left, I'm only going to the sub-PO, not the big one. That's it with the apples and stuff outside.'

He stopped the car and she let her seat-belt wind back into place.

'Don't suppose you're going to give me a lift back?'

He shook his head, wondering what her reaction would be if he suggested a date. The freckles spilled into a smile again. *Did* she fancy him? Copeland had thought so, and she certainly wasn't hurrying to get out.

Copeland. He took a quick glance at his watch.

She said, 'I'll be down at Gadfly's tomorrow, somewhere around nine o'clock. You can buy me a drink, if you like. Thanks for the ride,' and with a quick swing of her legs she was on the pavement and heading through the door of the shop.

As he drove away, he began to whistle cheerfully.

THIRTEEN

A THRUSH was singing somewhere at the bottom of the garden, repeating itself monotonously, and it was a measure of Morrissey's anxiety that instead of feeling relaxed by its song, he found himself annoyed by it.

It was a damp morning with just a hint of lingering ground frost in the sharp air, but the sun was already poking out sleepy pale fingers and there was promise of a brighter day. That alone would normally have been enough to cheer him, but not today. Today, not even the pleasure of being up and working in his beloved garden before the rest of the street was awake could help, and he tried to relieve his sense of frustration by thrusting the garden fork with savage force into the ground. It hit a stone. The jar sent wild signals through his arm and shoulder and he flung the fork aside.

'Sod it! Sod it to hell!' he said with quiet malice, and that didn't make him feel better, either.

The truth was that he couldn't get a 'feel' for the mind of the man he was hunting. A random killer, an opportunist, but not a sex killer, not yet. According to the police psychiatrist, that could change. According to the local paper, it didn't need to; if the victims were women, the murders were sexual.

He heard the paper-boy whistling on the other side of the hedge; the thrush grew silent, overawed by a more piercing virtuosity. Morrissey picked up the fork and began again, a relentless turning of earth, and when the border was dug he fetched the two boxes of bedding plants from the greenhouse.

The garden was his joy, his thinking-place, but not today. Today he couldn't make his fingers work through the soft loam without thinking of decay, and he set the young plants into their places doggedly, intent only on being done.

Margaret was in the kitchen and yawning when he went back to the house. Overhead there was a steady thud from Katie's stereo. If Mike were home, as he would be tomorrow, the sound would be overridden by arguing voices; Mike yelling for Katie to turn it off, and Katie goading him as only she could.

Margaret said, 'Don't forget to spread the word today.' He frowned. 'The market,' she chided. 'I expect a steady stream of buyers from the Malminster constabulary.'

Light dawned. The NSPCC stall. He'd forgotten that Margaret would be turning into a market trader for a fund-raising day. He said, 'And why does madam chairwoman have to be the stall person?' knowing she liked to be reminded of her relatively new status; having slogged quietly in the background before being elected to the committee, Margaret was now enjoying her reward.

'Because madam chairwoman enjoys standing in the market,' Margaret said cheerfully, 'and I'm not giving up my favourite perk. Do you want to eat before or after you change?'

'Better be before.' Morrissey reached to turn over the local paper that Margaret had been reading. As always, an uncaught killer meant police inefficiency. The headline shouted at him, 'MALMINSTER SEX DEATHS: WE SAY BRING IN THE EXPERTS' and beneath, in smaller letters, 'Cowardly Attacker Remains Free to Kill Again.'

Margaret put down the bowl of beaten egg. 'It's rubbish,' she said. 'How Neville Harding can take that holier than thou attitude in his position I don't know!' Her face had pinked with anger and for some reason it lightened Morrissey's depression. He put an affectionate arm round her, and she hugged him back.

He tried to sound severe. 'And what position is our local editor in that the ladies of Malminster know about and I don't?'

'Ah, well. The actual *position* is something we haven't found out, but everybody knows he has two homes going.' She ground pepper generously into the eggs. 'Of course no one mentioned it to Louise, and she's very loyal, but there you are. He's the last person to take a moral stance.' She squinted at her husband. 'Maybe you should tell him so. Just drop it into the conversation; ask after Natalie and watch his face.'

He studied her thoughtfully. Margaret and gossip didn't usually go together. Had the newspaper upset her that much? Then Katie came into the kitchen wearing a short cotton nightie that looked like an overgrown T-shirt. She collected a carton of orange juice from the fridge and a glass from its cupboard, and flopped on to a kitchen chair.

Her father sighed. Last year's black spiky Goth hair had grown into something resembling a hearth-rug which fell across her forehead.

She looked at her parents, and seeing Margaret's still pink face and Morrissey's cramped eyebrows, assumed a quarrel. Resting her hands on the table, she said, 'Back to bed, Katie. This is a war zone!'

Morrissey's hand came on her shoulder and kept her on the chair. 'There's no argument,' he said. 'Your mum's just annoyed at a lack of support for the hard-pressed fuzz.'

'Oh, how come?' Katie's eyes fell on the headline and she began to read, commenting, 'Stupid man. Probably keeps his brains in his underwear!'

Morrissey met his wife's eyes and saw his own amusement reflected. As he went upstairs to change, he was humming quietly.

LOUISE HARDING had been trying to keep up a brave front for more than a year, but it was increasingly hard, and at times she wondered what had ever possessed her to marry Neville. The only good thing to have come out of the union had been the children, but Nigel and Anne seldom came home, and Mark... It wasn't fair that Mark should have had so much taken from him, and she blamed herself for that; had always blamed herself and always would. It always came down to ifs... If she hadn't been in such a hurry; if she hadn't turned to wave to Anne; if she hadn't fallen down the stairs...

If she hadn't been so afraid of keeping Neville waiting.

The doctors had taken a different view and said Mark was lucky; he might not become a second Einstein but his brain could have suffered much worse damage from the lack of oxygen. And he'd done well, he'd coped with normal school, and if he had come from a different background, that minor achievement might have been enough.

But not with Neville for a father.

And then there was Natalie. She wondered what Neville was like with her; tender, caring, all the things Louise had given up looking for.

But there was one thing Neville was usually careful about, and that was other people's opinion. He liked to be well thought of in the circles that mattered, and until now that had meant not rocking the civic boat by risky comments in his newspaper. It was a shock for Louise to read the scathing headlines.

Why, she asked as her husband ate his breakfast, was he knocking the police when they were doing their best?

'Because I need to sell more papers to make more money,' he snapped. 'To keep you and him in the clothes you fancy wearing and food in your stomachs. It'd help if you stopped encouraging arty-farty ideas and told him to get a job. You can't make a horse out of a mule. I had to work my way up, and it's time he started.'

Mark was used to being 'he', and kept on eating. Louise wondered with despair if it hurt him never to be addressed directly by his father; it was one of the things she never dared ask. She wondered why there was that perversity in Neville's nature that made him deny that the son he was ashamed of had one bright talent. Mark had been given a place at the local art college not because of his academic work, but because of his ability to express himself on paper and canvas had demanded it. Under his fingers, the world he saw transformed itself into images that made Louise catch her breath. Perhaps it was a compensation for what had been taken away.

Anger swamped caution, and Louise cried in unaccustomed fury, 'If you weren't keeping Natalie dressed like a fashion-plate you wouldn't need to penny pinch! Why don't you tell *her* to economise?'

'If *I* earn it, *I* spend it, and I'll tell you this—she never has a headache.'

I bet she doesn't, Louise thought, but hers isn't a life sentence; it's day labour.

When his father was there, Mark's stammer was always worse. Sometimes, at college or alone with his mother, it was hardly noticeable, but with Neville Harding his tongue froze. As it did now. Mark knew about Natalie, and knew the difference between having a mind that worked slowly and being thick. Thick was what his father believed him to be. He made a special effort, 'Sh-Sh-She-She's screwing Bill Thompson,' he got out triumphantly. 'Na-Nat-Natalie,' and his father exploded.

Mark closed his mind and let the names wash over him. They didn't matter.

FOURTEEN

'UNLESS HE'S INVISIBLE,' Barrett said, exercising his ability to state the obvious, 'he must have left something of himself behind.'

'Too true,' accepted the chief inspector coldly. 'And I don't doubt Sherlock Holmes could find it; but I'm not that bloody clever. Are you?'

'At least we've found a link between Appleby and Susan Howarth,' Barrett replied huffily. 'And then there's the honeymooner in Acapulco.'

The thought of Acapulco reminded the sergeant of the freckle-faced girl, and Gadfly's. There'd been definite promise in the look she'd given him.

Morrissey spoiled the daydream. 'I want to know more about Sharon Nolan, and especially why she doesn't get on with her father,' he said. 'That should keep you busy for a bit.'

Barrett saw himself sent on yet another time-wasting exercise. Aggrieved, he protested, 'It'd hardly be Nolan. We know he wasn't nights off.'

Morrissey flicked the quibble away. 'Can Smythe ride a bicycle?'

Barrett shrugged. How was he supposed to know?

'Or Copeland, for that matter? Somebody will have to check how long it would take for Nolan to bike it from Middleton's, commit murder, and get back again. Just the first two; he'd have been at home when the Latimer girl died.' He fixed Barrett with a stern eye. 'And before you say anything, his wife wasn't at home. He's no alibi.'

'But that's only circum...' Barrett broke off.

'Yes? Only what? Circumstantial?'

'*Sir*,' said Barrett, caught out.

'I'll leave it for you to organise, then,' said Morrissey, his point made.

MORRISSEY LEFT for home at five-thirty and told Barrett to do the same. For the chief inspector there was nothing to be gained by staying at the office, and a lot to be said for hearing Mike's account of the three-day field trip to Gibraltar Point. But at the same time he was conscious that another day had gone without any real progress.

And Barrett had learned nothing from Nolan's daughter; his fears of wasted time had been correct. Sharon worked as a nursing auxiliary at the district hospital, and the sergeant's intrusion into a busy working day hadn't been appreciated by either her nursing officer or by Sharon herself.

She had inherited the angularity of her parents, but the softness of youth hadn't yet turned into disappointment. If she had been shorter, Barrett would probably have said she had a certain attractiveness, but since she was an inch or so taller than himself and refused to be intimidated by his rank and profession, he didn't bother to try out his charm. The result was that each found the other abrasive.

When he asked about her father, she was bluntly direct. 'You're off your trolley-wheels! Why the heck should I answer questions if you're not going to tell me what he's supposed to have done? Ask him! And anyway it's years since I left home. I don't know what he does with himself now.'

'That's the point, isn't it? What went wrong, why leave home at sixteen? No real need, was there?'

'It's not your business.'

'What about your mother, then? You still see her. I expect she talks about him—what he does, how they get on.'

'Then you'd better ask her, hadn't you? Not me.'

'Obstructing police enquiries...' Barrett had begun pompously.

'Obstructing my arse!' Sharon had cut across crudely. 'If he hasn't done anything, you've nothing to make enquiries about. Have you?'

And as he had been forced to report to Morrissey, that was as far as he'd been able to get. Barrett was still smarting from it when he went into Gadfly's.

The disco-bar was full of throbbing lights and loud music, and since he couldn't see the girl from Crowther's, he made for the bar. He had paid over the odds for a lager in a designer glass when he saw Michelle. The man she was dancing with wore white trousers and a shirt splashed with roses. Barrett blinked.

Smythe had advised, 'Wear something casual, forget the waistcoat and tie.' And Barrett had tried to do that; but his wardrobe hadn't yielded anything to compare with the bright oranges, purples and screaming greens that waved under the strobe lighting.

He turned back to the bar. There were only four years between himself and Smythe.

He was brooding on that when Michelle pushed in at the side of him. She seemed pleased, her smile wide as she clutched his arm and leaned against it. 'You've come, then. I didn't think you would. Are you going to buy me a spritzer?'

When it came, she dragged him away to look for an empty table. Barrett followed and found the noise increased until it reached a point where, when they sat down, it was impossible to communicate without yelling. Michelle didn't seem to mind, and Barrett tried to look as if he was used to it.

When they made a sortie on to the floor, he flung his pelvis around as best he could. Michelle looked approving, and he found consolation. Maybe there wasn't that much difference between himself and Smythe after all.

They were back at their table with two more drinks when the man with the red rose shirt appeared. He said, 'Shift up,' and pushed on to the bench seat next to Michelle, eyeing Barrett with hostility. 'I don't like being dumped.'

'You haven't been dumped,' Michelle told him. 'I wasn't with you, but I am with him, so push off.'

'Didn't know you were into stringy beef.' Red Roses leaned across the table and thrust his face into Barrett's. 'Got his own toothbrush as well.' He put his finger on Barrett's top lip and tupped his nose with it sharply. 'Is this what makes you fancy him, then? Is his moustache a turn-on like a French tickler?'

Barrett stood up, knowing he lacked a good three inches on his rival. 'Piss off,' he said pleasantly.

'Ah, go shave your pigging face.'

When Red Roses jerked up from the table, Barrett wondered what it would be, a fist or a foot, and when the foot came he grasped and twisted and enjoyed the crash that came after.

Michelle said, 'We might as well go now,' and slithered off the bench seat hurriedly.

A bouncer appeared.

He looked from the man on the floor to the unruffled Barrett, and said aggressively, 'What happened then?'

Michelle said brightly, 'He tripped up, didn't he? It's these stupid lights; they're too dim. You ought to do something about them. I mean it's dangerous, you could get sued.'

She flounced off. Amused and rather pleased, Barrett followed. As they went out, she grinned up at him. 'We can get a take-away and take it back to my place, if you like.'

Barrett liked.

KATIE HADN'T intended going home alone; in fact she had made a promise not to, but things changed. Once the row with Andy had flared, there was no way she was going to let him see her home, and she had stormed from the student union bar in a fine temper. Outside the college in the near empty streets, she had thought better of it, but by then it was too late for a change of heart; no way was she going back inside and risk looking an idiot.

Which was why, rather than wait almost half an hour for the last circular bus which would take her along Forest Drive to the stop near her home, she caught the bus to Brindley which would drop her instead at the north end of the Drive, where the roundabout gave access to the motorway.

As she took her ticket and went to find a seat, the doors hissed shut behind her then slapped open again to let another passenger on. It was the last Brindley bus, and the downstairs seats were almost full, with the windows steaming up gently and a boozy pub smell wafting around. As Katie sat down, she heard the clump of feet going upstairs.

When they reached the roundabout, half a dozen passengers got up, swaying with Katie along the narrow aisle to get off, and two men came down from the top deck, one elderly and patient on the bottom step, the other hidden except for his legs.

The downstairs passengers knew each other, walking on up the hill in a huddle, their voices loud. The elderly man walked past Katie briskly and turned into

Sycamore Grove. Turning the corner of Forest Drive, she looked for the other passenger, but saw no one. Perhaps he'd come down at the wrong stop and stayed on board after all.

The long tree-lined road stretched before her, curving to the right as it sloped gently downhill. The lights were less bright than on the main road, smaller, shorter versions of the dull grey concrete standards. Economy had decreed they be set on only one side of the road, leaving the other side, hers, with dark islands to be crossed. And one of the lights was out, making it even darker.

For the first time in Katie's life the Drive felt alien and she was reluctant to leave the bright corner. How stupid! It was her road, her home was half-way along, her mother would be waiting up for her, her father, too, probably. She remembered that Mike would be home from his field trip and stepped out quickly. It was only eleven and there were still a lot of people up; she wished their curtains were undrawn so that light would spill across the gardens on to the pavement.

A quarter of the way along, there was a soft footfall behind her. It wasn't something that would normally have caused her worry, but tonight for some reason her skin prickled. Too many dire warnings, she thought irritably, and then thought, with disembodied logic, that if she screamed someone would be bound to hear.

Two houses down from her, a big laburnum leaned out from the Jessops's garden and made a black cave.

A car came past and lit the Drive with its headlights, making Mrs Peeble's cat leap for the fence and safety. She recognised Tim Beal's Mini and wished he had stopped. But Tim was still sulking because she wouldn't go out with him.

The headlights ebbed away and the footfall came again, and this time it was closer.

She broke into a jog. There was nothing to be afraid of, she was almost home, and if there was anyone behind her, it was probably a neighbour going home like herself.

To prove her fear groundless she turned, and found it had been the wrong thing to do.

MIKE WAS UPSTAIRS in his room, but not ready to sleep until he heard his sister come in; it wasn't something he would have admitted, especially to Katie, but he had missed her. He had also missed his tape collection, and was laid on the bed listening to Pre Fab Sprout.

Downstairs, with one eye on Newsnight, Morrissey was also listening for Katie while Margaret read peacefully. He wondered why it was that fathers worried about daughters and mothers grew frantic about sons. It was he who heard the faint noise, and he who opened the door.

The sound had been like a dog scratching, but in the stream of light from the hall he saw it wasn't a dog at all but Katie, her face dark and mottled, her limbs jerking, and her eyes like swollen plums.

Katie!

He lifted her inside, feeling an aching tightness round his heart, and set her down on the carpet under the light, kneeling as he groped for his pocket knife, her head cradled. Margaret came and he leaned forward over his daughter, desperate that her mother shouldn't see until he had cut the cord.

He barked at his wife. 'Get an ambulance!'

'What . . . ? Let me see.'

'Damn it,' he said roughly. 'An ambulance. Do it now!'

When Katie was small, she'd had croup. Morrissey well remembered the harsh rasping followed by the high shriek of air laboured in. This was worse. Margaret remembered it too as she fled for the telephone and denied the urge to push her husband aside and see for herself.

Behind her, the chief inspector turned his daughter's head and set the blade of his knife against the knot. Neither he nor Margaret saw Mike standing in pyjama bottoms on the staircase shivering with shock.

BARRETT HAD BEEN making progress, and he wasn't best pleased to be disturbed. The remains of a takeaway from Kow-Loon's Chinese restaurant were still on the table, and he and Michelle were comfortable on a long-pile rug in front of the gas fire. That he had managed to dispose of someone taller and heavier than himself seemed to have impressed her, and Barrett intended pursuing his advantage. It was to that end that he was single-mindedly, but with apparent abstraction, undoing the buttons on her green satin shirt.

The keening note of his electronic pager spoiled the mood. He told himself that nothing could be that important, but had to telephone in just the same. As he dialled, he saw Michelle doing up her shirt again, and knew how Hercules had felt.

FIFTEEN

'I NEED TO SEE HER,' Morrissey said, and found himself measured by Lambert's sagging moonface.

'As a father or a policeman?' The ENT consultant didn't intend to be intimidated. 'Because Katie isn't in any fit state to answer questions.' Then he smiled charmingly at Margaret. 'Why don't you go through, Mrs Morrissey, while I bend your husband's ear.'

Margaret gave her husband a sidelong glance and went hurrying down the short stump of corridor. Guilt that she had been placidly reading while her daughter was attacked lay heavy on her mind, so painful that the illogicality of it went unnoticed.

Behind her, Lambert said, 'There's a lot of soft tissue damage and bruising, but that will heal. The damage to the larynx is a different thing, the compression caused internal bleeding. I shan't know how the vocal chords have fared until the congestion and swelling goes down, but I can tell you there's no chance of a squeak out of her tonight. I'd forbid it, even without the state of shock.'

Morrissey said flatly, 'A nod or a raised hand might be enough.'

'No. And in any case I've had her sedated,' said Lambert. 'I'm sorry. See her as a father, and leave the policeman outside.'

Huddled in the corner, Mike stirred and shuffled his feet, forgotten. The waiting-room was small, with half a dozen chairs and a low table. The handful of magazines were dog-eared with use. He coughed, and the sound reminded Morrissey he was there.

'Mike.'

His son leaned forward. 'Can I see Katie, Dad? *Please*?' There was the smallest hint of panic, and Morrissey picked it up, then he saw how pale Mike was and the red-rimmed eyes, and remembered that his son had seen Katie at the worst point. He let the policeman slide away from him.

'As a father,' he promised Lambert. 'Nothing else, not tonight.'

WHEN MORRISSEY took his wife and son home there were arc lights set up along the road, and the commotion had brought on most of the house lights round about. House-to-house enquiries were almost completed, and so was the painstaking search of road and pavement. Barrett detached himself from a knot of men, and came hurrying.

When Margaret wound down her window, he ducked his head and leaned on the door, looking in at them worriedly. 'They searched outside the house first, so you can take the car up. How's Katie?'

'She'll survive,' Morrissey said shortly. 'I'll be out in a minute.'

Barrett stepped back and let the blue car sweep past him, getting a tired smile from Margaret as it went. He watched Morrissey usher his wife and son inside the house and saw the lights go on, then the chief inspector came back down the drive, long legs moving quickly, arms flapping loosely as they always did when he felt things might be getting away from him. He stood with Barrett, watching the search. Although it was April, there had been three nights of hard frost and the ground was white with it. He felt the cold snap at his fingers and thrust them into his pockets.

'Anything?' he asked abruptly.

'Not much. There seems to have been a scuffle of some sort two doors down where the laburnum leans out. There are twigs broken off as if someone had been grabbing at it.'

Katie trying for a weapon? Morrissey wondered. Something to use in self-defence.

'If he attacked her there, she'd have had to crawl,' he said. 'From there to the door, over the gravel.' He didn't think she could, not so far.

'There are marks on the lawn, something dragging.'

'My lawn?'

Barrett nodded and walked with him, back through the open drive gates. Although the frost was thickening, the damaged grass could still be seen. Long scuff-marks; Katie trying to come home? And then having to cross the sharp gravel at the end, cutting her legs.

After the frosty silence in the gardens, after the agony in stony places ... He let the robot part of his mind occupy itself with Eliot, and thought of Katie's legs.

'He dragged her,' he snapped in sudden loud anger. 'Hell, Neil, he dragged her home and left her! The backs of her legs were cut—not her knees. The bastard knew she was my daughter.'

Barrett felt some of the chief inspector's shock communicate itself. He struggled with the new idea. 'Then he knows a lot about you,' he pointed out. 'More than just a name. Appleby could find out things like that; he'd have the right contacts.' His face showed eagerness again.

And Nolan, Morrissey thought, was there a way he could know too? A clever monkey searching the Electoral Roll.

Barrett kept after his own hare. He said, 'I sent a patrol car round to check on Appleby's house. The Sierra was in his drive, with the bonnet still warm.' He half expected Morrissey to dismiss it, and he did.

'Half the car bonnets in Malminster would be warm at that time,' he said. 'But thanks; it was good thinking.'

The sergeant admitted, 'Nolan is nights off. I sent a car round there, too, but the house was in darkness. Could have been in bed or out on the town, so I told the driver to hang around for a bit.'

'No luck?'

Barrett shrugged. 'Control sent him off to a break-in.'

Morrissey's mind slid back to his daughter. When he left the hospital she had been deeply asleep, her breathing noisy. Lambert hadn't known if the swelling would increase. If it did, there would have to be a tracheotomy and Katie would hate that; it would leave a permanent scar on her throat to remind her of a madman. He wondered again if she might hold the slim clue that could end the case. She was the only one to have seen her attacker and survived. She could tell them about him. *If and when she was able to talk*? He sighed. The best he could do for now was leave a WPC by her bed.

The arc lights began to go out.

Suddenly weary, the chief inspector said, 'You've done a good job, Neil. I'll see you later at the office.' Barrett nodded and turned back to the road.

As Morrissey went back into his home, the unwelcome thought came that now the case could be taken off him; Osgodby could say there was personal involvement.

And that made him angrier still.

THE CHIEF INSPECTOR hadn't slept well, and when he woke, there was a sour taste in his mouth and a sour feel to his mind. Light was seeping round the edges of

the curtains and the clock at the side of the bed said
six-thirty. He thought Margaret was asleep because
her eyes were closed, but when he turned back to the
bedclothes to ease himself from the bed, she opened
them, blinking at him.

He said, 'I'll bring you a cup of tea. Stay in bed
awhile.'

'Only until you're out of the bathroom. I want to
get back to Katie.'

'There's Mike,' he reminded her. 'Give him a
chance.'

She said, 'He can go round to Martin's. I'll ring
and make it all right for him.'

'Perhaps he won't want that,' Morrissey pointed
out gently. 'He's too old to be baby-sat; you'll have
to let him decide for himself.'

Her face looked as if it were about to crumple. 'I
want to know he's safe.'

'He will be. Trust him.'

'I do,' said Margaret bitterly, sitting up and swinging her legs to the floor. 'It's the bloody world I don't
believe in any more. I'll wash my hands and put the
kettle on.' She thrust her arms through the sleeves of
her cotton robe and pulled it angrily tight, scraping at
her hair with a brush before sweeping out of the bedroom. Morrissey let her go, knowing she had to work
off her anger somehow, before it ate too deeply and
became fixed.

And there was still anger there from last year, from
the aftermath of the killings at Little Henge.

He heard Margaret's feet on the stairs and took her place in the bathroom, laying out his shaving things carefully. There was something else, too, although Margaret would never say it out loud. A feeling that he had in some way failed; that he, a public guardian of law, should at least be able to keep evil from his family. But the idea itself was an illusion, because he couldn't always be there to protect; there was no magic umbrella to keep them from being rained on.

As he soaped his face he heard a click from the telephone extension and guessed that Margaret would be dialling the hospital. When the same sound came again, he went downstairs half-shaved to learn what they said. Some of the strain had gone from his wife's face. He said hopefully, 'Good news?'

She nodded. 'It didn't get any worse. They didn't need to operate.' Morrissey sent up quick thanks to a God he professed not to believe in, and Margaret said, 'We've been lucky, haven't we, that Katie's still alive? I'm not going to think about what it might have been.'

'Best not to,' the chief inspector said gruffly. 'Not when she's going to be all right.' He bent to kiss her, and she saw the lather and backed away.

'Shave,' she said, and they grinned at each other.

He left the house at seven-thirty and called in on Katie on his way to work. A white dressing covered the deep rawness where the ligature had dug deeply into her neck, and there were bluish-red patches above it that crept over on to her face, small petechial

haemorrhages where capillaries had swelled and rup-
tured. She looked pale and very young. Morrissey had
an urge to lift her from the bed and sit with her in his
arms, as he had on countless occasions when she was
small. But Katie wouldn't thank him for it now; it
would only offend her newly emerging adulthood.
Instead, he sat on the bed and gripped one hand in
both of his.

The policewoman displayed tact, and with a quiet,
'Excuse me, sir', went out of the room. His daughter
gave a shadow smile and moved her lips, but no
sound came. He saw a small spark of fright in her
eyes.

'It's all right; no lasting problem,' he reassured her.
'A few days, and you'll be able to yell at me as loud
as ever. Promise.' The fear went. He said, 'If you remember anything about him, anything at all, write it
down for the WPC.' She nodded, and that hurt her
too. He stood up. 'Your mum will be here when she's
organised Mike, and I'll be in to see you later.' He
kissed her forehead and smoothed the rug of hair.

The policewoman had placed herself strategically
at the end of the short corridor, and when he left Katie's room, she came hurrying back.

He said, 'If she comes up with anything, I want to
know right away. Keep a pen and paper handy for her.
Make sure your relief knows to do that, too.'

He waited until she was back in Katie's room before he turned and made his way through the maze of
hospital corridors to his car.

He didn't think his daughter would be ready to face the thought of her attacker just yet, and intended to see her again when he'd spoken to Lambert and knew it would do no harm to question her. But Katie surprised him. Just before nine-thirty, and on his way to answer a summons from Osgodby, he was called back to the telephone.

The WPC's voice said breathlessly, 'It's a message from your daughter, sir. She's written, "Tell Dad he smelled like an old ash-tray." '

Morrissey remembered the stale tobacco smell in Appleby's office, and the way he opened a window to let the smoke escape. He said slowly, 'Tell Katie: Thanks, that's a big help. It fits someone we've been looking at. Let me know if there's anything else.' He set the receiver back in its cradle. Too many things now were beginning to point to the sales manager. He looked at Barrett thoughtfully. 'Take someone along with you, and ask Mr Appleby if he'll be good enough to come back with you and answer a few questions.'

Barrett got up eagerly. 'And if he doesn't agree?'

'Lean on him,' said Morrissey and moved to the door.

The telephone rang again, and Barrett picked it up. He looked at the chief inspector doubtfully. 'For you again,' he said. 'Someone with information for your ears only. Sounds dodgy, like a heavy breather.'

Morrissey sighed and came back. A man's voice said with rough thickness, 'I could have killed her if

I'd wanted, right on your own sodding doorstep, Morrissey.'

The chief inspector covered the mouthpiece. 'Trace it!'

As Barrett moved at a trot out of the office, Morrissey took his hand away and forced his voice to take on neutrality, pushing the image of Katie away. Time enough for anger when the talking was done. He said, 'I don't know what you're telling me.'

The laugh that came back held no humour. 'Oh, you bloody know, all right! Shall I tell you where I am, then, save the bother of tracing it?'

'Now listen . . .'

'No. *You* listen! 'Course you want to know where I am. Wouldn't be stupid enough to tell you, though, would I? Better watch it, Morrissey. That daughter of yours was lucky, but if I have to meet up with your wife sometime . . . Well, think about it. I wouldn't be that kind twice. Miss her, would you?'

Kind. Morrissey flinched. *Miss her*. He said, 'Why don't we meet and talk about it? Anywhere you like. Just you and me, if that's the way you want it.'

'Doing your best to keep me talking. Listen, go on TV again and mouth off about me being a coward, and you'll wish you'd cut your fucking tongue out. Down to you, Morrissey, it'd be one less bitch.' The line went dead.

Barrett came back, and shook his head. 'Not enough time,' he said. 'Was it good information?'

Morrissey stared at him, agate eyes hard and deep with new anger. 'It's been taped?' he demanded curtly. 'That, at least?'

Barrett nodded, waiting to be told what it was about.

Blackly the chief inspector said, 'If he's to be believed, that was our random killer.'

'Appleby?'

'How the hell do I know!' Morrissey barked. 'That's to find out when you bring him in. So do it.'

SIXTEEN

OSGODBY WAS behind his desk, and worrying. He spun the chair so that he could reach the coffee jug behind him. Morrissey took the offering silently. A cup wasn't a good sign; a mug was the thing that showed comradeship in the chief super's office. Cups were for VIPs or the condemned.

'Brief me on last night,' Osgodby said, and leaned his elbows on the desk.

The chief inspector was careful. 'Katie was attacked on her way home. She's in hospital, but recovering. There's good reason to suppose it was the man we're already looking for. If it is, it could be his one mistake.'

Osgodby pricked his ears. 'You've got something new?'

Morrissey said, 'I'm hoping there will be when Katie can talk to us. One strong pointer has come out of it already.' He recounted her relayed message and the fact that Appleby was being brought in. Then he added, 'But don't read too much into that. I'm not personally convinced it's him, but there are too many fingers pointing that way now to let me ignore them.'

When the chief superintendent drummed on the blotter and sucked his teeth, it was a sure sign of stress. 'John...'

'We're getting closer.' Doggedly the chief inspector went on. He balked at discussing the call he had just taken, but it had to be done, and the reaction was as he had expected.

The fingers gave up their drumming and steepled. Osgodby distanced himself. 'A personal vendetta is out, John. Too many people still remember the phony letters and tapes in the Ripper case. We can't afford to look in the wrong direction.'

'My stepping out of it now won't be any help,' Morrissey argued. 'He's been rattled, and that's always good.' He leaned forward and put his head on the same level as the chief superintendent's. 'The important thing about the telephone call is that we have a voice-print; and genuine or not, it came from somebody who knew what happened last night. The fact it happened to Katie isn't going to cloud my judgment. You know me better than that.'

'And you know the regulations, John.'

'Yes, I do. I know they can be tailored to fit.'

Vexed, Osgodby said, 'It'd mean clearing it with the CC; full and frequent reporting.'

'If that's what it takes,' agreed Morrissey with meek accord.

The chief superintendent looked at him suspiciously. An amenable Morrissey was unknown and disconcerting. He began to shuffle papers. 'I'll let you know,' he said abruptly, and Morrissey felt he had won a minor if not a whole victory. Osgodby would hate calling in help from outside the division, and no one inside had enough seniority to take over.

Except the chief superintendent himself.

He was reminded of that when he got back to his own office and found the telephone ringing.

Osgodby said, 'About Appleby. Let me know when he arrives. I want to sit in. No objections, have you?'

Yes, thought Morrissey. Loud, strong, noisy objections, but he didn't voice them.

APPLEBY DIDN'T TRY to bluster. Morrissey took that as a good sign, then asked himself why. The objective was to prove guilt, not look for indications of innocence. He put himself next to the man and twitched his nose, getting the scent. A faint smell of tobacco stimulated his olfactory sense. Very faint. Not the smell of an old ash-tray.

They were in the larger of the three interview rooms, and Osgodby had already chosen his place, near, but slightly back from, the table. Barrett had moved a chair to its left, and was setting up the tape-recorder.

Appleby's eyes ran round the plain cream walls, his expression neutral.

Morrissey said, 'If you wouldn't mind sitting down, sir. There are several things you might be able to help us with.'

Appleby sat, and said with a wry grimace, 'Helping the police with their enquiries. It sounds intimidating and very damning.'

'Your presence here is entirely voluntary,' Morrissey said. 'I'm sure Detective Sergeant Barrett pointed out that you can have a solicitor present if you wish.'

'He mentioned it. I'll waive the right until later. The fewer people who know I'm here, the better. Mud sticks, as they say.'

'Then we'll see if we can sort it out between us,' Morrissey said. 'Tell me again where you were on the fifth of February, the eighteenth of March and the ninth of April.'

Appleby sighed, and went through it all again.

Morrissey said, 'Let's go back to February fifth. You took a day off because your wife was ill. Did you stay in the house with her all day?'

'No, it was a 'flu bug. She spent the day in bed, and in the afternoon I went down to the library and exchanged some books for her. On the way back I called at a florist's and took some flowers home. That always cheers her up. Between times, I cooked the meals. Although when I say "cooked", it might be an exaggeration—heated up a few tins and packets would be nearer the truth.'

'But you were home that evening?'

'I had a Rotary meeting. Gwen insisted I go. She felt better by then, so I didn't see any reason not to.'

'What time were you home again?'

'About eleven.'

'And the Rotary Club meets where?'

'Beechwood House.'

'In Beechwood Park?' Appleby nodded. 'A girl was murdered quite near to Beechwood House that evening.'

'Yes, I know, but we heard nothing. With the windows closed, the rooms are practically soundproof; we went through it all at the time. We were all questioned. You must have the reports somewhere.'

'Let's move on to March fifteenth, then. You'd been to a sales conference in Durham, is that right?'

'I left home at six-thirty in the morning, and got back about eleven-thirty at night. I would have been home earlier, but I had to change a wheel.'

'You drove up the A1?'

'And the A1(M). And I travelled back the same way.'

'Straight home?'

There was a pause. Appleby admitted unwillingly, 'I sometimes pick up a Chinese take-away on my way home. I did that on March fifteenth.' He stared at the chief inspector. 'From Kow-Loon's.'

Morrissey stated quietly, 'Diane Anderson died that night between ten and twelve on a scrappy bit of rough ground behind the cinema. You know where I mean: where the old back-to-back terrace row stood. They pulled it down to build a skate-board park. Now it's just weeds and rubble. Not a nice place to die.'

'I had nothing to do with it.'

'Kow-Loon's is just round the corner.'

'I had nothing to do with it.'

'And on the ninth of April between one-thirty and two-thirty. Where were you then?'

'In Malminster, trying to find an anniversary present.'

'Any luck?'

There was something very close to dislike now in Appleby's eyes. 'None.'

'It's less than a ten-minute drive from Crowther's to the common—sure you didn't go home for anything?'

'Quite sure.'

'Or park anywhere near the common?'

'I'd have got bloody wet!' Appleby snapped. 'It was teeming.'

'So it was. Did it worry you when the umbrella went rolling down the hill?'

'What umbrella?'

'Would it surprise you if I said a Sierra like yours had been seen parked near the common?'

'No. Quite frankly it wouldn't, there's a lot of them about.'

'You knew all three girls, Mr. Appleby. Susan Howarth, Diane Anderson and Gail Latimer. And you were in the vicinity at the time of all three murders.'

'I was nowhere near the common!'

'We only have your word for that.'

'Then it will have to be good enough.'

'Gail Latimer had a boyfriend called Rob. Your middle name is Robert. We're coming up with a lot of coincidences.'

'I think,' said Appleby, 'I'd like my solicitor here now.'

'If that's what you want,' said Morrissey. 'But I'd like to ask one more question. Where were you last night between ten-thirty and eleven-thirty?'

'My solicitor,' said Appleby. 'Graham Standing. I'll speak to him now, if you don't mind.'

SEVENTEEN

OSGODBY SAID, 'On the surface, we have enough to make a formal charge.'

Morrissey admitted that the chief superintendent was right, then he argued, 'But it's all circumstantial, and I don't like that. If we could establish a motive, something less flimsy than his middle name being Robert, I'd be a lot happier. And there's nothing.'

'What about the Sierra parked near the common?' Osgodby said.

'What Sierra?' Morrissey shook his head. 'I said "what if", just in case it would spook him, but it didn't.'

'If we charged him, it might shake something out,' said Barrett. Moodily he turned a pencil end over end between his fingers. 'Except that now he'll have his solicitor with him.'

'When Standing comes off the golf course,' Morrissey agreed. 'Until then, he's held on suspicion, and until something changes, I think that's enough.'

'Well, it's still your case,' said Osgodby, 'and no one can say you're leaning too heavily.'

Morrissey sat solidly and gave nothing away. It wouldn't do to let Osgodby in on the simple fact that if his hunch told him Appleby fitted the frame, he would lean on the sales manager very heavily indeed. He remembered how Katie had looked, helpless on the doorstep. *Very heavily*.

Osgodby said, 'What about the other man—Nolan? He was the Latimer girl's stepfather, wasn't he?'

'Foster parent,' said Morrissey. 'He could have had the opportunity, he's got a bike and I don't doubt he could get out of his workplace without being noticed; especially on the night shift. Motive is different. We know Appleby had met all three women; the only one we're sure about with Nolan is Gail Latimer. I think it might help if we let on to the local news media that we're looking for a man named Rob. The usual thing. Tell them it's to eliminate him from our enquiries.'

Barrett stopped playing with the pencil and looked at him. 'Bit late, surely, sir?'

'Someone in Malminster may have seen them together. We need that person—or persons—to come forward.'

Barrett looked slightly mollified.

Osgodby said, 'I'll pass it through, then, and let out we're holding a man for questioning. Principle of give the dog a bone.'

Morrissey wondered how long it would take to get Standing away from his round of golf, and tried to ignore the gut feeling that in the end it wouldn't matter one way or the other.

IT WAS ALMOST one when Appleby's solicitor arrived and demanded to see his client alone. By then, Morrissey had been back to the hospital and left a list of questions for Katie to answer. 'Take them slowly,' he had advised the WPC. 'Give her time to remember.'

But it could be nothing else but slow with Katie needing to write down the answers.

Margaret had been with their daughter, looking a fixture. Both had looked glad to see him.

Now he was back in his office with an egg and bacon butty lying uneasily in his stomach, and Barrett still downstairs in the canteen.

The telephone rang, and when he heard Matthew Haines's voice he remembered Tracy Lambton and the school medicals.

Haines said cheerfully, 'I thought I'd let you know the Nolan foster child's been moved.'

Morrissey came upright in his chair. 'Interference?'

'Don't know about that. The school doc went into a huddle with the social worker, and I got word this morning that Tracy had been moved from my catchment area. The social worker is Carol Phipps from the Queen Street office, if you want a chat. How are the rest of your problems?'

'Growing,' said Morrissey. 'Thanks, Matt, I owe you.'

'Any time,' said Haines. 'By the way, we keep having to clean rude graffiti off the outside walls. Mostly Monday mornings.'

Morrissey grimaced. 'I'll ask uniform to keep a closer eye for a bit,' he promised, and sighed as he put the phone down. It rang again before he took his hand away. Appleby was ready for another talk.

This time, Graham Standing was there, and when Barrett started the tape-recorder, he said with firm formality, 'I have advised my client that there is no legal necessity for him to give you any information at all. He feels that he has already offered all the help he possibly can.'

'Remaining silent can be misconstrued,' Osgodby said.

Standing dismissed that. 'From what Mr Appleby has told me, I don't believe he claimed the privilege of silence.'

'We've covered most of the ground,' said Morrissey. 'There's only one question Mr Appleby declined to answer. I'd still like him to tell me where he was last night between ten and twelve.' Standing looked at his client, and Appleby shook his head. Morrissey continued, 'I'm sorry there seems to be a problem with that. If his presence in a particular place could be confirmed, it would save us all a great deal of trouble, and not least in that, your client himself.'

Appleby said, 'Where I was couldn't affect any part of your investigation, Chief Inspector. I'm sorry I can't be more help, but I should really like to go home now.'

Morrissey was regretful. 'I'm afraid that isn't possible, sir. You were formally cautioned this morning, before our first interview began, and we have the power to detain you while we make further investigations. Because of the seriousness of possible charges, we must exercise that power. Unless, of course, you can offer some proof of your innocence for the relevant times.'

Standing said quickly, 'It isn't for Mr Appleby to offer proof of innocence, Chief Inspector. It's for you to provide proof of guilt.'

'Exactly. Which is why your client will be detained in police custody while we pursue enquiries.'

Appleby looked shaken, and his face lost colour. He sought reassurance. 'Graham . . . I haven't been arrested?'

'They have a right to detain you for questioning.'

'Gwen won't know what to do.'

'She can spend the night with Beth and me.'

'The night?' Appleby's voice rose. 'Good God, you don't mean I'm stuck here until morning?'

'Tell us what you were doing yesterday evening between ten and twelve, and it's possible we might release you,' Morrissey offered.

Appleby stared at a point on the wall above the chief inspector's head, and said tonelessly, 'I have nothing further to say.'

AT TWO O'CLOCK the local radio news-reader gave out that a man was being interviewed in connection with the three murders. He also said the police would like a man named Rob, who had been a close friend of

Gail Latimer, to come forward. The next bit of information hadn't been authorised, and Osgodby was livid. Now all of Malminster knew that the method of strangulation had been three strands of green garden twine. All three items were repeated on the local television news bulletin and picked up by the evening paper.

Listening to the radio as he drove had become a habit with the vulpine-looking man, more so now that he himself was mentioned so often. He was trapped in a slow-moving stream of traffic on the Middlebrook Road when he heard the news bulletin, and at first it amused him so much that they had the wrong man that he had to pull in until the paroxysm of laughter passed. Then anger took over. They had no right to say that, to tell his method. *How* he worked was between him and Morrissey; putting it out like that let any tinpot exhibitionist have a go.

He swung right, across the path of an oncoming car, and got a prolonged blast from his horn. His arm swung out of the open window with fingers spread in a vicious V.

At a telephone on the Coronation council estate, the only Telecom box that hadn't been vandalised, he called Morrissey and swore at him for having caught the wrong man.

This time, so great was his sense of injustice, so intense the cold, unemotional anger, that the chief inspector managed to keep him on the line long enough for the call to be traced. But by the time a Panda car pulled up alongside the yellow and black box the receiver was dangling free.

Three boys in their early teens were hanging around the bus shelter across the road, and when the police driver asked if they had seen the man using the telephone, they nodded. Asked which way he had gone, all three pointed in the opposite direction, and as soon as the police car was out of sight they brought out a can of red spray-paint and began to decorate the shelter with four-letter words.

MORRISSEY HAD BEEN on his way out when he took the telephone call, and it had disturbed him. This time it had been recorded from the beginning, and for the first time he felt he had some faint idea of the mind of the man he was looking for. *If* the caller and the killer were one and the same.

Hunches weren't enough to go on, not with Osgodby peering over his shoulder. Until something broke, he had to remain carefully methodical.

The search warrant for Appleby's house had come after Katie remembered something else about her attacker: he had worn yellow rubber gloves.

'The kind found in every kitchen,' Morrissey grumbled before they began to comb through the house. Between them, he and Barrett found six pairs, and to the chief inspector it seemed a futile exercise.

But Barrett felt differently. He it was who discovered a pair in the potting shed next to a part-used cone of green garden twine.

Gwen Appleby was in floods of tears when they had finished, and Morrissey blessed the fact that he had brought a WPC with them. Remembering what Graham Standing had said, he rang the solicitor and checked that Appleby's wife wouldn't spend the night alone.

It was almost eight when he returned to the hospital to sit with Katie. His daughter's eyes were red, and it was obvious that swallowing was an agony for her; each time the need came, her hand lifted to her throat as she tried to ease the pain.

Morrissey's hands bunched on his knees. He said, 'I will find him, Katie, I promise you that.'

She reached for the pad of paper and pencil, and he waited patiently while she scribbled. He read, *Tim Beal passed me in his Mini.*

'On the Drive?'

A tiny nod. She wrote again. *Only a minute before.*

Morrissey sighed, and bent to kiss her forehead. 'You're a clever girl,' he said gently. 'I'll go and have a word with young Tim. If he wasn't spliced out of his mind, he should have seen who was coming up behind you.' He squeezed her hand and moved away.

As her father went out, Katie's face screwed up again at the memory of who that had been.

Tim's mother looked surprised to find Morrissey on her doorstep, and then distressed that he wanted her son. The chief inspector said quickly, 'It isn't anything he's done; just someone I hope he may have seen last night. Did a policeman call on you?'

'Yes, of course, all the houses,' Madge Beal said. 'I saw the lights and commotion, but nothing before that.'

'And Tim?' asked Morrissey. 'Had Tim seen anything?'

'I don't think so. He came in and went straight to bed, and his room is at the back of the house. He had to catch an early train this morning; he's hiking with two friends. Somewhere Bolton Abbey way.' She looked unhappy. 'I'm sorry, but he won't be coming home until late Monday. I hope it isn't important.'

'It isn't anything you need worry about,' sighed Morrissey, and went home.

That night, while Morrissey worried intermittently and Appleby lay uncomfortably in the cells, another woman died.

EIGHTEEN

It was seven-thirty in the morning and Appleby looked haggard, a fact that pleased Barrett as he set up the tape-recorder again. If he felt as bad as he looked, he would be that much nearer to giving them the real facts and getting off his high horse.

Morrissey wasn't so sure. In Appleby's place, and if he were innocent, it would have brought out a fine stubbornness. His eyes took in the rumpled suit and skin, the hand that kept going to a side pocket and coming away empty, and took pity on the man.

He said gruffly, 'If you're out of cigarettes, I'll have some brought in.'

Barrett looked at his chief in shocked amazement. Appleby was rattled as a hare with two hounds, so why offer cigarettes to calm the man's nerves? This business with Katie must have really loosened Morrissey's nuts and bolts. He coughed and raised his eyebrows.

Morrissey, interpreting the message, felt irritated. He said tetchily, 'Stick your head out, Neil, and have someone fetch a pack of cigarettes and three coffees.'

The patting hand relaxed, and Appleby said, 'My position hasn't changed, Chief Inspector. I haven't anything else to say.'

'Not even in your own interest?'

Appleby shook his head, and Barrett came back from the door, looking smug.

Morrissey tried a different approach. 'Your wife must be worried sick,' he suggested. 'If you can prove where you were and what you were doing the night before last, why not think of her?'

'I was doing nothing illegal, and Gwen is very much in my thoughts.' He shifted. 'Don't you have to let Standing know you're interviewing me?'

'If that's what you want.'

'It's what I want.'

Three mugs and a pack of Silk Cut were brought in on a tray. Appleby reached for the cigarettes.

Barrett said sadistically, 'If you're not going to talk to us, you won't have time to smoke, will you?'

'A cold turkey cure?' Appleby tore off the cellophane, then his hand stayed. 'No matches.'

Morrissey produced a lighter from his pocket and saw a flicker of gratitude. 'We don't enjoy detaining innocent men,' he said.

'Then let me walk out?'

Barrett said, 'When the evidence points the other way? You must be joking.'

Morrissey put the lighter back in his pocket. 'I'm trying to be fair, Mr Appleby, but you seem to want to damn yourself.'

'I have nothing further to say,' Appleby repeated.

A PC came and whispered to Morrissey. The chief inspector stood up and nodded at the tape-recorder. 'Suspend it,' he instructed Barrett, and deliberately set his lighter on the table again before he went out.

Gwen Appleby was in one of the interview rooms, and Graham Standing was with her. She had obviously taken care with her make-up, but she hadn't managed completely to hide the dark arcs below her eyes that clearly spoke of a sleepless night.

When Morrissey came in, she turned to him and said in an anxious rush, 'Chief Inspector, I know why you've detained Brian, and I know where he was on Friday night.' She flapped her hands helplessly. 'It's such a mess! And he doesn't think I know about it.' Now she hugged herself. 'He visits a massage parlour. I followed him once—I have my own car, you know—and I saw him go in.' She looked defiant, the abstracted, scatter-brained air he had seen before gone in the face of something that demanded her full attention. 'And now you're wondering how I knew it was that kind of place? The explanation is that I work weekends at the special clinic, Chief Inspector, and the girls, there are three of them, come in for regular checks. It was the address he went to, you see; I knew the address.'

Standing said, 'This is very difficult for Gwen— Mrs Appleby. I suggested that you might have no need to tell her husband where the information came from.'

'Wives aren't usually so loyal or so understanding in these circumstances,' Morrissey pointed out.

'But you don't know the circumstances,' she said, sounding quietly sad. 'And if you did, you wouldn't find it surprising.'

'I don't believe my client's reason for being there should interest you, Chief Inspector,' Standing pointed out. 'The crux of the matter is that he was.'

The chief inspector agreed with him, but human curiosity being what it was, an explanation would have been welcome.

Standing proffered a slip of paper, and as Morrissey took it, Gwen Appleby said in a low voice, 'I suppose that kind of business is illegal?'

Morrissey said, 'Yes, I suppose it is, but there are always casualties,' and went to find if anything was known about number 7 Prentice Street.

OSGODBY'S UNHAPPINESS showed. He said, 'All right. If he didn't leave there until eleven, he couldn't have attacked Katie. But it doesn't clear him for the other three.'

'I think it must,' Morrissey argued. 'It might go against the grain to let him go, but the ligature round Katie's neck was identical to the other three. For my money, it has to be the same man.'

'Three strands of garden twine—everybody knows that now.'

'But they didn't on Friday night.'

The chief superintendent gave in. 'All right, release him. We can always pull him in again if we need. Make sure he knows he can't go anywhere.'

Standing and Gwen were waiting for Appleby. Morrissey watched her arms go round her husband before they walked away together. As they got into Standing's car, he speculated on their personal problems. Would they, he wondered, get worse or better without Prentice Street?

Grateful that such things hadn't played any part in his own marriage, he went home to eat a civilised Sunday dinner with his wife and son, and afterwards he drove them to the hospital.

There was no policewoman in Katie's room today, but PC Hicks had the task of sitting outside in the corridor.

When he saw Morrissey, he leapt to his feet and saluted. 'Sir.'

Mike, coming up behind with his mother, grinned.

Katie was feeling better; that much was obvious as soon as they walked in. Instead of lying limp and pale, she sat up against her pillows, and when she saw Morrissey she waved her pad of notepaper.

He reached out a hand. 'You've remembered something?'

Mike tried to read over his father's elbow, and got shoved away. 'Police business,' Morrissey said severely. 'Not to be gossiped round Fisher Comp.'

'Do I ever?' Mike complained, but he went to sit on the bed without any more urging. 'I brought the travel Scrabble, if you feel like it,' he said off-handedly.

Katie's hand was a generous scrawl, easy to read. *Not sure, think I was followed from bus.*

The chief inspector looked at his daughter with fond disapproval. 'Did you see him?'

Katie's head moved slowly sideways, and she waggled her fingers for the pad. *He came downstairs behind elderly man from Sycamore Grove.*

Morrissey sat on the bed and gave her a hug. 'Katie, you're a wonder, but you've given me work to do. Sorry, love, I'll have to go.'

Margaret said, 'I knew it was too good to last. Do you think you'll get back?' She studied her husband's face, and got her answer. 'Never mind,' she sighed. 'I should know better than to ask.'

IT WASN'T IN Barrett's nature to give up an idea gracefully, and after Appleby had been released, his mind played around the possibility of collusion in some form. But when he couldn't come up with any good reason for three women to give up a steady income just to provide a middle-aged sales manager with an alibi, he put the whole thing on a back burner and went to the canteen. Later, when the sense of anticlimax had lessened a little, he telephoned Michelle's flat.

Michelle was pleased that Barrett wanted to see her again. They'd got to a very interesting point before he left on Friday night, and she still hadn't decided just how far she would have let him go. He had a much smoother technique than anyone else she'd been out with, probably because he was older, and she was eager to test it again.

Not that she intended to make that obvious to him; the siege was infinitely more exciting than surrender.

THE MUNICIPAL CEMETERY had been planned, and the ground bounded and made over, in the nineteenth century, when the fashion for monoliths and stone angels was at its zenith. The larger the monument, the more worldly goods the corpse it covered had amassed. Knowing that travellers into the town wouldn't like to be reminded of their mortality, the town fathers had built a high brick wall to screen the cemetery from the main south road. Its entrance was from the narrow and ill-lit Honeypot Lane.

Pedestrians tended to avoid walking along the lane past it after dark, and because of that, it attracted a lot of parked cars. Every so often the beat policeman would take a young constable along and shine his torch through the steamed-up windows, totally disrupting the courting couples' pleasure. Then, for a few nights, the lane would be almost empty.

And because everyone knew about Honeypot Lane, the odd scream went unremarked.

Saturday night had been dank and chill, and when Morrissey had left his home to interview Appleby again on Sunday morning, there had been a steady

drizzle of rain. Just before one o'clock the sky grew
lighter, and by two a watery sun was half-heartedly
poking through the overcast. The woman who lay so
awkwardly between the blackened stone spire of John
Henry Oldroyd's resting-place and the graveyard wall
hadn't noticed any of it, although her eyes were open
to the rain that washed them. With nothing left but
eternal patience, she waited to be found.

NINETEEN

MORRISSEY'S RETURN to division headquarters with a quick step and a look of anticipation was noted. It caused mild excitement. The buzz was that something new had come up. The chief inspector reserved comment.

He knew Sycamore Grove well, it lay behind Forest Drive, a small cul-de-sac of semi-detached houses, newer and less solidly built than those on the Drive. Morrissey hoped the poor weather would have kept the occupants at home. He sent out a half a dozen uniformed men with questionnaires, and waited, not expecting the whole exercise to take much over an hour. When the rain stopped he wondered if it were a good omen.

At the other side of town, Charlie Harmsworth was glad to see the rain clear because it was Nellie's birthday. The newspaper-wrapped bunch of late daffodils he carried in his hand were from his garden, the bulbs planted in the autumn, before Nellie died. It distressed him that she had never seen them in full bloom.

To reach his wife's grave he had to walk along the wide path between the old monumental tombstones. On the left a single row of them stood between the path and the tall brick wall, on the right they stretched to the opposite side of the cemetery, and through them the weak sun poked nosily among shadows and reflected from wet grass.

Charlie's eyesight was now less than perfect, and if the shoe had been black or brown he would probably have passed it without seeing it. But it wasn't black or brown, it was bright turquoise. Muttering irritably about litter-dropping vandals, he moved to pick it up and drop it on the rubbish pile. Then his eyes focused better and he saw that the shoe was on a woman's foot. Edging down the fringe of grass that separated John Henry Oldroyd from a grime-encrusted angel, Charlie saw the rest of her, and had to lean hard on the monument until he had recovered enough to go and tell somebody.

WHEN BARRETT ARRIVED at Michelle's flat, she was wearing a pink jump-suit. She accepted the chocolates he had paid exorbitantly for at an off-license shop, and allowed herself to be kissed in exchange. Barrett took that as a good sign and made himself at home while she put the kettle on.

'I usually curl up on the settee on a Sunday and watch TV,' she said when she came back. 'But we can do something else if you like.'

'Curling up sounds good to me,' said Barrett, and pulled her down beside him.

'I didn't mean *that*!' she giggled, only half trying to wriggle away.

He nibbled her right ear. 'I did,' he promised, and his pager began to bleep.

'It has to be a mistake,' he said as he picked up the phone. 'It just has to be a mistake.'

MORRISSEY KEPT his hands in the pockets of his raincoat. Even in high summer there always seemed to be a dank chill in graveyards and today, with an edge on the skittering breeze, everyone was trying not to shiver. The photographer had finished his work, and the SOCOs in their disposable white overalls were waiting for the pathologist to finish so that they could begin.

The chief inspector was pessimistic. He didn't think they would have a lot of success. In a panic, Charlie Harmsworth had stopped the first thing he had seen on the road. The bus carried only six passengers and a driver, but once Charlie had made himself understood, there had been a mass exodus, and God knew what they'd touched, and disturbed, and trampled on before the first Panda car arrived and moved them to a safe distance. Soon after that, alerted by one of the same bus passengers, a reporter from the *Malminster Echo* drove up, and not much later, by some strange filtration process, an outside film unit from the local TV station came.

The SOCO team had put up green canvas screens, and white tape now kept watchers at a distance, but the damage had been done.

Barrett said grudgingly, 'Well, Appleby's in the clear for this one.'

'Glad you realise that,' Morrissey returned shortly, and sank his chin against his chest. They'd wasted time on Appleby. Then he asked himself what difference it would have made; they'd had nothing else to follow up.

He shifted impatiently, watching Warmsby back out delicately from behind the grave. A laurel leaf stroked a wet band across the bald head, and the pathologist put up a hand and rubbed it away. 'Don't know why you let Jim Reed move out of the district,' he complained. 'Coax him back. It'll save time.' But he was half-smiling as he said it, knowing that Reed, an ex-pathologist turned GP, had got what he wanted; a country practice. He said, 'Last night some time, hard to be precise. Twelve to twenty-four hours is the best I can offer. Age about twenty-five, bottle blonde, garrotted with garden twine.' He blinked. 'Heard about your daughter. Bad business. Any closer yet?'

'A needle in a haystack would be easier,' said the chief inspector.

'Well, you can move this one when you want; handbag's underneath her.' He looked at the sky. 'I wanted to get the lawn cut today.' He began to walk away. 'Might as well get the PM over with instead.' He ducked under the white tape, fending off reporters, and hurried for the gate, shaking his head.

The SOCOs moved in and retrieved the handbag. Inside, undisturbed, were credit cards, chequebook and wallet, carrying the name Natalie Parkes.

Natalie!

Morrissey remembered Margaret's Friday morning comment about Neville Harding. *'Ask after Natalie, and watch his face.'*

The chief inspector thought about that as he watched the dead woman being zipped into a body-bag, considering the possibility that if this were the same Natalie, he would find himself doing just that.

CREDIT CARD COMPANIES and banks were not the easiest people to prise information from on a Sunday, but because nothing in the dead woman's handbag held an address, it fell to Barrett to persuade someone to open up their files. Since the chequebook was from a Malminster bank, he tried that approach first.

The manager twittered that it was highly irregular and very inconvenient, and he had house guests. Couldn't the whole thing wait until Monday morning; it was after all only a matter of hours? He wasn't best pleased when Barrett said snappily that one of the bank's customers had probably found getting murdered rather inconvenient too. Stiffly the manager agreed that he would open up the bank.

With Barrett so occupied, Morrissey had time to look at reports from Sycamore Grove. Katie had been right. At number 18, a retired bus inspector had travelled home on Friday night on the Brindley bus. As always, he'd sat upstairs. Somewhere in the back of the chief inspector's mind, a positive sixth sense stirred and stretched.

Cedric Stanley had said he remembered the passenger who had followed him down the metal stairs at the roundabout, because the same man had only just caught the bus as it was pulling out of the bus station. A drop-out type in John Lennon glasses; not young, though; not a teenager despite the jeans and camouflage jacket. Hard to see much of his face under the green woolly hat and straggly hair, but yes, he thought he'd know him again. And he smoked roll-ups.

Enough for a photo-fit.

Morrissey found DC Smythe doing slow typing again, and sent him instead to ask Cedric Stanley if he was willing to help them establish a photo-fit likeness.

OSGODBY HAD expected to spend his Sunday evening at home and was ill-humoured in Morrissey's office. He said rattily, 'If there weren't so many bloody spending cuts, there'd still have been a caretaker or whatever they used to call him at the cemetery. Perfectly good little bungalow there going to waste because the council can't afford to pay wages. Same with the gates. Nobody to lock them, so they stay open all night. But why the hell anybody'd want to go into that sort of place to canoodle, I don't know.'

'We don't know what she did,' Morrissey said. 'She could have been dumped there after death; the PM should show that one way or the other.'

'Expect it to, do you? Ever hopeful? Bloody will-o-the-wisp like last time; four now, five with your Katie, and we've come up with nothing.'

Morrissey gave him the news about Cedric Stanley, and some of the anguish went out of Osgodby's eyes. The chief superintendent savoured the idea of a photo-fit. 'Sure about that, are you? Because I'll tell you, you're lucky, John. You've only got me on your back; I've got the CC screaming for blood, and at the rate we're going, it'll be mine.'

'I'm hopeful,' said Morrissey ambiguously.

'Try for certainty,' said the chief superintendent, and went heavily up the stairs to his own office.

BARRETT CAME BACK with the address they needed, and he and Morrissey were going out through the swing doors when Smythe came in with Cedric Stanley. It wasn't a case of the chief inspector taking time out to make himself known; instead, he had his hand pumped in an astonishingly strong grip for someone so sparely built and pensionable.

'No need for names,' Stanley said. 'Not when you look just like you did on't box. And me and you working together, eh? That'll be something to drink on for a bit! Happen I'll be on next. That'll be a turn-up!'

'Especially if you can give us a good likeness,' Morrissey reminded him.

'Oh, that's no worry. Photographic mind for faces, ask our Hilda. See somebody once—it never goes. It's a knack; some folks have it, some folks haven't.'

Smythe said, 'Photo albums?' and Morrissey nodded, hoping Stanley hadn't planned to do anything that evening because there wouldn't be much of Sunday left when they were finished with him.

Barrett wanted to know what it was all about.

Morrissey said, 'More from Katie's memory. Her attacker possibly travelled on the same bus with her. And, if we're lucky, Mr Stanley can give us a description.'

'About time we got a breakthrough,' complained Barrett, his mind flitting back to Michelle.

Malminster was a town of many parts. Park a car for too long on the Coronation estate and hub-caps had a habit of disappearing; by contrast, a walk past the tall Edwardian villas edging two sides of the cricket ground made the air itself feel expensive. Some of the houses had been converted into flats. Natalie Parkes had lived in one of them.

Morrissey had keys from the dead woman's handbag but, not knowing if she lived alone, he knocked before he used them. The hall was minute, but the rest of the flat was airily high ceilinged, with ornate plaster cornices. It had one bedroom, furnished in dark pine, and a small bathroom and kitchen that were both bright and functional. The sitting-room ran the length of the house and the window at each end made it a place of light. It held a slight air of disorder without there being any evidence of it.

At the far end, where the window looked out over a rear garden, a round ash table and four chairs stood on a circular Afghan rug. A matching rug, oblong in shape, lay across the front of a cast-iron fireplace that had had a gas fire built in. Two black corduroy chesterfields faced each other across a long coffee-table.

The front window, a wide bay with a padded box seat, gave a direct view of the cricket ground. Against the long side wall a run of waist-high cupboards and drawers matched the ash table and gave space to an assortment of pot plants, books, a pile of magazines and pieces of ceramic. Nothing in the room was expensive enough to match the rent that would be paid, except possibly the Afghans.

Did someone pay it for her?

In the kitchen, one cup, saucer and plate waited on the draining-board; in the bathroom, one toothbrush sat alone without male toiletries edging it for room. But the shelves inside the bathroom cabinet looked accustomed to holding more than they did now. As though another person had already removed all traces of themselves from the flat.

Barrett felt it, too. 'Something missing,' he said.

Morrissey guessed that in this part of Malminster people minded their own business, but a regular visitor to Natalie's flat might have been seen and remarked upon. With that in mind, he sent Barrett to ask questions at the ground-floor flat, and while he was gone used the car radio to ask for the SOCO team. He needed something else, too: addresses to match two numbers he had found in Natalie's telephone index; one next to an underlined 'Nev', and one next to the word 'Mum'.

He wasn't surprised to learn that 'Nev' and Neville Harding shared the same telephone number, but the second address, when it came, brought him to the worst part of his job; breaking news of a death was never easy, and murder only increased the horror of it.

THE CHIEF INSPECTOR took a policewoman with him to visit Natalie's mother, and felt relieved beyond measure to find there was also a father, and that Natalie was not an only child. And then he had to ask William Parkes to identify his daughter's body in the hospital mortuary, and watch the man's shoulders bow under the weight of it.

Now the autopsy too was ended, and Morrissey and Barrett were in the small post-mortem room adjoining the mortuary where Warmsby held Natalie Parkes' brain between his hands with an almost careless casualness. 'No damage,' he pointed out for the second time to the chief inspector. 'And that means chummy's changed his MO. The first three had been concussed, probably with a fist, *before* they were garrotted.' He set the brain back in a stainless steel bowl and squinted at Morrissey. 'Are you getting my drift?'

'I think so. I'm not sure I like what you're telling me, though.'

'I didn't expect you would,' said Warmsby, and moved back to the table. 'And you've seen her fingernails, broken, all of them. This one put up a fight, and from the angle of the knot, he was behind her. Three strands of twine—but not plaited. A different ligature.' He picked up a curved needle trailing a length of silk and began to sew the scalp back into place.

Barrett, tinged green like the theatre gown he wore, said, 'You haven't put the brain back.'

'That's right,' said Warmsby. 'She isn't going to need it, and it's a good specimen.'

'Looking for a man with scratches,' said the chief inspector, 'is something to go on.'

The pathologist shrugged. 'My guess is she was scrabbling at his hands, and he probably wore gloves. I doubt she could have reached far enough to get his face. That's my guess, anyway. We'll know for sure when forensic's had a look at the nail-parings. Deciding why he's changed tack is your job, but she didn't die in the churchyard; distribution of hypostasis suggests lying curled on her left side for at least an hour after death; probably in the boot of a car. And,' he held the needle still, 'She'd had intercourse just before. Forensic got a comb-out, so you might be luckier with this one. He seemed to have been in a hurry, and careless.'

'If that's the good news,' said Morrissey with heavy resignation, 'let me do without the bad.'

TWENTY

IT WAS NINE-THIRTY and already dark when Morrissey and Barrett went back to Natalie Parkes's flat. The SOCO team had left, and a police driver waited patiently in his patrol car with the keys.

There was a different feel to the flat now, as if the influx of strangers had disturbed its identity.

As Morrissey examined the possibility of lover and killer being one and the same, Barrett, squatting before a cupboard, asked, 'How thorough are we going to be?'

The chief inspector looked at the jumble crammed inside. 'How dead is Natalie?'

Barrett sighed, and began to sort through the clutter. He knew it wouldn't help. Sorting through the other three's belongings hadn't done anything. Except turn up that damned estate-agent's leaflet. *Rob!* Maybe she'd invented him.

Morrissey found the photograph album in her dressing-table, filed with snaps of family and friends and some of Natalie herself at different ages. One that was obviously recent showed her at a party in an off-the-shoulder dress. The man with her looked faintly familiar, but it certainly wasn't Neville Harding. On the back, someone had written, *BT, New Year party*.

Morrissey lifted it from the page and put it in his inside pocket. When they left, he took the telephone index with him. And he worried, as Barrett drove back to division HQ, about the empty spaces in the bathroom cabinet.

Margaret said, 'Yes of course I remember talking about Neville Harding, but I thought you didn't like gossip?' She moved a pan from the cooker and emptied it into a wide-necked flask.

Morrissey sniffed. 'What's that?'

'That,' she said screwing the cap down firmly, 'is something I should have thought of before. Soup; for when you tell yourself you're too pressed to grab something in the canteen.'

'There are times,' Morrissey said humbly, 'when I think I don't deserve you.'

'There are times when I know it,' answered his wife. 'But I don't let it keep me awake at night. What do you want to know about his girlfriend for?'

'I thought you might know her surname, the local ladies' grapevine being what it is.'

Margaret scowled at him. 'Thanks! And I didn't notice any of Malminster's finest at the charity stall. That came up on Friday morning, too.'

'And I forgot, I'm sorry. Did you make much?'

'A hundred and forty-nine pounds.' She sat down and buttered a piece of toast. 'Natalie Parkes. Now tell me why you want to know?'

He said. 'Because Natalie Parkes died some time on Saturday night.' He saw his wife's shocked look, the quick assumption made that Natalie had been number four, and felt guilty not to say that this was probably a copy-cat. But he hadn't said that to anyone yet, not even Barrett, although, with all the facts available, the sergeant should have worked it out for himself.

Margaret was thinking about Katie, and how closely death had brushed her by. Morrissey said, 'There was a mention of it on last night's news, but she hadn't been identified then, so they didn't have a name.'

'I didn't put the television on—or, at least,' she looked faintly embarrassed, as if caught out, 'Mike and I played computer games. And don't laugh.'

'I'm not laughing,' he said as he put his jacket on. 'I just hope you didn't let him win.'

She smiled. 'I think it might have been the other way round,' she admitted. 'Repayment for all those games of Ludo.' The smile went. 'Why do I get the feeling it's going too fast? Katie's grown up, and Mike will be gone before I've caught my breath. It isn't intimations of mortality that bother me, it's intimations of an empty nest.' She glanced at him. 'Now you're going to tell me it goes with the territory.'

Not always, Morrissey thought. There were parents who hated their children for growing up and showing them how they themselves once were, and could never be again. But he didn't need to remind her of that; working on the NSPCC committee, she had learned it for herself.

He could tell her that children never really left home, that they always came back; that there would be grandchildren filling the place with laughter and sound again, but it wouldn't necessarily be true. Guilt assailed him. It was almost a year since he'd been back to Settle, since he'd taken Katie and Mike to see his parents. When this case is over, he thought, when I can turn round ... He picked up the flask. 'We love them and they love us,' he said gruffly. 'Anything else is up to Providence.' He bent to kiss her. 'Who knows—we might have to prise them out of the door.' But that was a lie, too, and Margaret would know it. 'It'll be a late night again, don't wait up,' he reminded her, and went out to his car.

Upstairs, Mike leaned his elbows on the bedroom window-sill and watched his father drive away.

NATALIE PARKES had worked as an optician's receptionist in North Street, that much Morrissey had found out from her parents, although neither of them knew whom she was going out with. Morrissey hadn't liked using the euphemism 'going out', but it was gentler. If he needed to, he would use the world 'lover' at a different time. Without much expectation of anything helpful, he sent Barrett and Smythe to collect whatever belonged to the dead girl from her workplace, and to find out whatever they could from people she had worked with.

Perhaps she had a confidante there.

Meantime he had to face the chief superintendent again, and Osgodby, who had shown himself to be good at organisation and administration but had never lit any beacons during his time in CID, had the files relating to the four dead women upstairs in his office, and was sucking on his teeth again. He was feeling a mite happier now that the photo-fit had been released, and had told the assistant chief constable confidently that with all off-duty and leave cancelled and the streets of Malminster policed to capacity, it should only be a matter of time.

But Morrissey spoiled the mood by pointing out, 'We don't actually *know* this man followed Katie home.'

It was unwelcomingly negative. Osgodby dismissed it. 'Difficulties for the sake of it,' he said. 'That's what you're doing now. Get a copy to Katie and see what she says. There must be a policewoman spare if you're busy.'

And then the telephone on his desk rang, and it was Susan Reed wanting Morrissey. She had decided to tell him about Rob.

'You see?' said Osgodby. 'It's all starting to come out.'

It was another dull day and the common looked bleak and grey when the chief inspector pulled up outside the terrace of houses. Susan Reed was fidgetty, wandering round the flat touching things, picking up and putting down, and he wondered when she would get to the point. When she did, it was something he hadn't expected.

She said in a rush of words, 'There isn't a man called Rob—there never was. You've been looking the wrong way. I suppose the ring she wore made that damn leaflet seem more important than it was. I should have found it before you came, then it would never have seemed important at all.'

Morrissey forbore to ask what ring, and watched as she struggled with a silver band on her own right hand. When it came off, she handed it to him. 'It's the same inscription as Gail's,' she said.

He held it between thumb and forefinger and saw the spidery letters. *Gail-Rob*. 'Just like hers,' Susan Reed said in a kind of desperation, 'except the other way round. Susan Robina Reed, Chief Inspector, that's my full name. I suppose you'd call me a bull-dyke, but it's a bloody awful name. That's the way men think, though, isn't it?'

Some men, thought Morrissey, and some women too. To be different was always dangerous.

'I wish you'd told me before,' he said, suddenly staring up a blind alley. He didn't tell Susan Reed that the murdered girl hadn't been wearing a ring.

Had it been lost or stolen? The thin wolfish face of the night mortuary attendant came into his mind, and he sighed.

Sidetracks were a bloody nuisance.

TWENTY-ONE

THERE WERE three council estates in Malminster, and at different times the man Morrissey wanted so badly to find had lived on them all. The flat he occupied now was on the sixth floor of a ten-storey block, where the concrete stairwell was covered in graffiti and smeared with other things that were worse.

The pocket radio on the squalid kitchen window-sill crackled with static, but through the hiss and muted thunderflashes of sound he heard about the cemetery murder. The news item punched through his throbbing head as he fed himself with Paracetamol tablets. For a while, the throbbing became worse.

He hadn't killed on Saturday night. He hadn't been anywhere near the cemetery.

Wanting a mug, he found they were all in the sink. Everything was in the sink! Groping, he located what he needed, and swished it under the tap.

At different times during the morning he tried to ring Morrissey, and each time had to hang up because the chief inspector wasn't there. The injustice of it grieved him.

Near one o'clock he parked behind a pub off the Brindley Road, where a pint of bitter and a beef and pickle sandwich cost one pound fifty. The bar television was turned on to the local station, and when the photo-fit came on, the landlord said, 'Bloody fucking bastard,' and leaned on the bar confidentially. 'Trade's down ten per cent,' he complained bitterly. 'Women won't come out. I'd like to swing the bugger by his balls.'

Nodding, his mouth full of sandwich, the man he was talking about took a swig of bitter and watched the rest of the news.

THE CHAIR outside Katie's door was empty, and the door itself stood part open. Hicks was on the far side of her bed where he could see the door without turning, the chair he sat on tilting forward as he moved a chessman. When Morrissey came in, the impulse to be upright was automatic, and the chair teetered as it gave way to gravity.

'Sir!' said Hicks, waiting for the reprimand. Two chess pieces slid to the floor.

In the sigh of a croak, Katie said, 'Oh, Dad!' The reprimand died. Hicks righted the chair and moved out of the room.

As Morrissey grinned fondly and inanely at his daughter, part of the black cloud he had walked under since Friday shifted and went away. 'Shouting already!' He gave her a hug. 'Sounds good. Feel up to looking at a photo-fit?'

He wondered how she would react to a sight of the man, if it would upset her, but she looked at the picture with detachment.

'Ever seen him before?' Morrissey asked.

The 'no' caught in her throat and in exasperation she grabbed the notepad and wrote *WEIRD*, underlined with thick scribble.

Her father nodded. 'He's no Mel Whatzisname, that's for sure,' he said, thinking of the poster in Katie's bedroom and forgetting the name. A ghost of her old grin flicked into place.

He'd half-expected tears, hysterics, or a drawing away into silence when she saw the face and connected it with the man who attacked her, but instead she was in command of herself. Relieved at that, but disappointed at the lack of recognition, he put the photocopied face back in its envelope and bent to peck her cheek.

'I'll be back when I can,' he said, and she put her arms up and hugged with the fierceness of a five-year-old.

Out in the corridor, Hicks was still on his feet. Morrissey said sternly, 'Better finish the game, but don't make it too much of a habit,' and went his way.

He got into his car not knowing that when Katie moved her black bishop, its facelessness did what the photo-fit had failed to do. With memories of the attack swamping her and her face twisted in panic, she began to gasp and claw at her neck. At the brink of a panic of his own, Hicks rang the bell. When the nurse got there, Katie was sobbing into the young PC's shoulder, and he, with his arms around her, knew he liked that position very much.

By the time Morrissey arrived back in his office, Osgodby had already left for a meeting at County Force Headquarters, a fact that didn't displease the chief inspector.

Barrett was ostensibly writing up notes, but at the same time he wondered how to bring up that which was troubling him. To his mind the first three murders had been opportunist, but the cemetery murder had been planned, and it stood out a mile. Nothing about it fitted the pattern, and it worried him that the chief inspector hadn't said so, too. He cleared his throat and carried on writing.

Morrissey said, 'Anything come out of the optician's?'

Barrett pulled a long face. 'Nothing useful. I collected her personal belongings and brought them back, but there's nothing but make-up, pens and loose change. As far as people go, there's a second receptionist, two opticians and an optometrist, all reckoning she's going to be missed, but they'd say that anyhow, wouldn't they? It's the only perk there is to being dead. I asked about boyfriends, and didn't get much joy there, either; they knew she'd been seeing somebody who wasn't short of a bob or two, but couldn't or wouldn't put a name to him. This BT on the photo seems the likeliest bet; I sent Smythe to hurry up the telephone numbers.'

Morrissey nodded. 'And?'

'And what, sir?'

'You tell me,' said the chief inspector, knowing his sergeant well enough to recognise when there was something needing to be got off his chest. He wondered why Barrett was holding it back. If he'd known it was because Barrett thought Morrissey hadn't worked out all the probabilities he would have been amused, but as it was he sat back and waited, hearing the black leather chair creak as it took the strain. Last year they'd tried to fob him off with a new and flashier model to match the refurbishings, but Morrissey had out-finessed them in the end.

'Sir...'

'Yes, Neil?'

'It's this last murder. There's too many differences in MO; it's like we're not looking for the same man.'

'And you worked that out yourself, did you?'

Barrett looked put out, and answered stiffly, 'Seems a reasonable hypothesis, sir, given the differences in method.'

'I'm glad you picked up on it,' said Morrissey. 'And you're quite right: there's mistakes all the way with this one.'

The sergeant's face cleared. 'Somebody she knew,' he said eagerly. 'Somebody trusted, who could get behind without making her nervous. A boyfriend.'

'Or someone she thought was harmless,' the chief inspector suggested. 'There's that, too.' Smythe came in with the list of names they were waiting for, and Morrissey took it.

Barrett said, 'It's the garden twine that makes the biggest difficulty. He could have picked up about it from either the local news on Saturday or the evening paper, but in either case if he wanted to copy-cat he'd have had to run out and buy some, or he had a ball handy. Whichever way it was, it didn't leave much time to plan; but I get the feeling it *was* planned, if you see what I mean.'

The chief inspector regarded his sergeant with a feeling of affectionate surprise. Barrett had been using his brain. He was reminded that the leak about garden twine hadn't been authorised, and no one had done anything about it yet.

It was something he thought Smythe could usefully occupy himself with. He said, 'Off you go down to the Press Office with my compliments and find out who leaked that little tit-bit about the twine. And when you've found that out, ask who got to know first. Lean as hard as you like, and make sure they know I'll be leaning myself if they don't come clean.'

Smythe moved his buttocks from Barrett's desk. To lean with official blessing would be a new experience.

There was something that Barrett didn't yet know, but Morrissey waited until the DC had gone before telling him, rightly guessing what the sergeant's response would be.

'I learned a little something myself this morning,' he said. 'From Susan Reed. We can stop chasing after Rob, because there's no such animal.' He told Barrett what he had learned, and watched the sergeant's face change from disappointment to anger.

Barrett exploded. 'I can't believe the amount of wasted time asking questions about a dyke!' Morrissey looked regretful; Susan Reed hadn't been far wrong. 'Are we sure she's not lying?' Barrett went on. 'Covering up for... No,' he shook his head. 'No, I'm not going down that road again.'

'I'm glad to hear it,' the chief inspector said. 'And don't be so narrow minded. I thought yours was supposed to be the thinking generation, the live and let lives.'

'Some of us grew up,' said Barrett stiffly. 'What about the missing ring? Do you want me to check it out now?'

'Make sure it isn't listed first,' said Morrissey, already certain himself it wasn't. 'If not, find out what time the page three fancier comes on, and take Smythe with you when you question him.' His eyes went back to the list of names and addresses the DC had given him, each linked with a number from Natalie's telephone index. 'Ever watch Malminster R.U. play?'

'Not recently.'

'I thought not, or you'd have recognised their full-back on Natalie's snapshot. We'd better hope he doesn't give us any arguments, or you could be in trouble.'

From his greater height, and with shoulders that could match any rugby player's, Morrissey smiled benignly.

TWENTY-TWO

'I WAS COMING to see you anyway,' Bill Thompson said as he led them through his sports shop. A wide-eyed assistant watched them pass, and the customer she was serving didn't take pains to hide his curiosity. They followed the rugby player into a cramped stockroom at the back of the shop, crowded with football boots and trainers on high shelves, with cardboard packing-cases taking up the rest of the floor space. At the side of the door an ancient desk cowered in the corner with two sorry-looking wooden chairs. Morrissey eyed them with distrust, and stayed on his feet.

Thompson said, 'It was a shock hearing about Tally that way, over the radio. I'd seen her not that long before, at least... I suppose not long, not if she died Saturday night.' He stared at Barrett's notebook. 'Longhand?' he said with detached interest. 'Must be hard keeping up if you get a fast talker.'

'I'm a fast writer,' Barrett said with equal detachment. 'What time did you say you saw Natalie Parkes?'

'She came down to the game Saturday afternoon and went back home with me afterwards. That's become a fairly regular event with home matches; I wish I'd persuaded her to stay; she'd have been safe then.'

'What time did she leave?' asked Barrett.

'Nineish.'

Morrissey said with politeness, 'How close was your relationship with Miss Parkes? Close enough to have had intercourse before she left?'

Thompson eyed the chief inspector. 'What the hell has that got to do with the police?'

'A lot of things. The act in itself is innocent, and we can find out in other ways if we have to, so why not just a straight yes or no?'

'Tally didn't just sleep around; it wasn't like that at all. I'd been seeing her since Christmas, and I wanted her to move in with me, make it a permanent thing, but she had things to sort out first.'

When Thompson hunched his shoulders and tucked his chin into his neck, Morrissey had a glimpse of what the man would be in another twenty years, when the muscular flesh was wavering into fat. It was a disturbing reminder. He pushed harder. 'One way or the other, I have to know. Did you have intercourse, sir?'

'Yes,' the word was toneless. 'Yes, we did, and then she left to meet someone else.'

'Who?'

'I don't know his name. A businessman she'd been seeing for a year or more, but she was going to finish with him. We'd talked about it, and that's what she'd decided. I do know he was married and fairly loaded, because she let it slip that he'd set her up in her flat.'

'You quarrelled about that, did you, sir?'

'No, I bloody didn't—it was before I knew her.'

'But it must have rankled, not knowing who he was,' said Barrett. 'Knowing she went from you to him. Unpleasant. Enough to make anyone angry.'

'I told you; she was going to end it with him and come to me.' Thompson half sat on the desk, and it squealed and shifted slightly. The dark colour was gone from his face and his mouth set in a straight line.

Morrissey didn't doubt the misery in the man's eyes was real enough; the only question was if it was all sorrow or part guilt. 'What did you do when she left?' he asked. 'Did you walk her into town, drive her— follow her?'

'Tally had her own car; she left in that.'

Barrett swapped looks with Morrissey. He said, 'I suppose you can give us the make and colour. And the registration number.'

Thompson said, 'A black Panda, 237 DWY. Two or three years old. E, I think.'

'Did she give you a lift, then?' said Morrissey. 'Into town, perhaps?'

'I drove myself,' Thompson said. 'Down to the clubhouse, had a few drinks, a couple of games of pool, something to eat, and back home.'

'And no doubt a lot of people saw you there?'

'No doubt they did, but where is it all leading?'

'What make of car do you drive yourself?'

'A Montego estate.'

'Nice car,' said Barrett. 'Parked round the back, is it?'

'That's where I left it.'

Morrissey said, 'Do you use a valeting service or clean it yourself?'

'Neither. I run it through the car-wash.'

'Done that today, have you?'

'Yes, I have. Why, is it a big issue?'

'I should like you to let me have your car keys...'

'What the hell for?'

'...And to let us have the car taken into the police garage for examination. It will be returned in pristine condition.'

'No,' said Thompson. 'No, I'm damned if I will! I'm not going to be marked down as a suspect. God, it's ridiculous! I'd as soon break a leg as hurt Tally.'

'You could be damned if you don't,' said Barrett. 'We can move it with your co-operation or with a warrant, but move it we will.'

Bullishly scowling, Thompson folded his arms.

Morrissey said, 'Better to get it over with, don't you think? Settled.'

'No, I don't. Last time I saw Tally was nine o'clock. You'll have to look somewhere else for who killed her.'

'First we need to eliminate you. What time did you say you left the club?'

'Just after midnight; I gave Kenny Hawkes a lift home.'

Barrett said briskly, 'What address?' and got another scowl.

'Oakwood Lane, 24. I watched the end of the ITV
horror film with him and left about half-past one.'

He took a set of car keys from his pocket and laid
them on the desk at his side. 'I don't know what
you're looking for, but you won't find it in my car. I
need it to go to the wholesaler's on Wednesday.'

'We'll be through by then,' Morrissey promised,
and hoped they would. 'Did Natalie Parkes tell you
where she was meeting this other man?'

'Back at her flat.' Morrissey saw Thompson's eyes
flicker, and wondered if it was because he'd just re-
alized the other man in Natalie's life could be her
killer, or if it was something else; a moving away from
his own guilt, perhaps.

'We won't keep you any longer,' Morrissey said,
and Barrett picked up the car keys and put them in his
jacket pocket. 'But I'd like to know how well you
knew Gail Latimer,' he added.

Thompson had begun moving to the door, now he
stood still. 'I didn't,' he said, and let his anger hang
out. 'I didn't bloody know her at all.' He went out
into the shop, leaving them alone.

MORRISSEY TOOK the first phone call just before one-
thirty as he sat at his desk and dunked a bread roll
into a cup of Margaret's soup. He recognised the
voice straight away and hoped it had been recognised

in communications, too, but made signals to Barrett just in case.

The caller was aggrieved, and the aggravation came across clearly. 'Look,' he complained in Morrissey's ear, 'that girl in the cemetery had nothing to do with me. I don't want anybody putting out it had, not unless you'd like me to pay another visit to that ripe little plum of yours. There's no hurry; I can wait till she's out.'

It took a while for Morrissey to cork his anger enough to speak, and he recognised that failure as the kind of personal gut reaction Osgodby had been afraid of. When he did speak, his voice was rough round the edges. 'Let's meet and sort it out. Just the two of us.'

'Nothing to sort. Three are mine; this one isn't.'

'Same method,' Morrissey said.

'After you bloody splashed it everywhere, it would be, wouldn't it? Maybe I'll not wait, after all. Saw your wife today, Chief Inspector, busy washing her car she was. Nice-looking woman.' The line clicked and went into the disengaged signal.

Barrett came back, and shook his head. 'Not enough time.'

Morrissey dialled his home, hoping to God Margaret would be there and knowing there was no reason for her to be. He was ready to give up when she answered.

'Sorry, love,' she said cheerfully. 'I was washing my hair.' Then her voice changed, and she said quickly,

'It isn't Katie, is it? Mike and I are going to see her when he comes home.'

'No,' Morrissey lied, 'nothing to do with Katie, I just wanted to hear a friendly voice. Bet you washed the car today, too, didn't you?'

'Psychic again?' She laughed. 'This morning, actually. Did someone see me?'

'For me to know and you to wonder. You're remembering what I told you about keeping doors locked . . .'

'And not letting strange men into the house. Yes, of course, but I'm not going to be made a prisoner, either. If I'm outside, I'm well armed with a garden fork, so don't worry.'

'I'll try not to,' he answered drily, and felt better when he hung up.

The second call came as he put the receiver down, but this voice was immature and polite when Morrissey gave his name, saying, 'You don't know me, sir, but I'm Colin Swift and I live in one of the houses at the bottom of the common, across from the bus shelter.'

'Yes,' Morrissey encouraged him. 'I know the ones you mean.'

'Well, the thing is, I take a lot of photographs, and I thought you might be interested to see some of them that I took the day there was a murder.'

Morrissey sat up straight. 'I very well might,' he said. 'Are you going to show them to me?'

'If you'd like to come and see me, because I can't come to you. Mum won't like it. I wanted to talk to you before, but she wouldn't have it. Anyway, she's had to go out for a few minutes and she doesn't know I'm talking to you, so when you come, don't let her put you off, will you?'

'I promise you I won't,' Morrissey said gravely. 'Which house is it?'

'Number 12. I'll wave to you from the window. Will you come now?'

'About fifteen minutes,' Morrissey said.

'That's all right; she'll be back by then, otherwise there wouldn't be anyone here to let you in.'

'But there'd be you,' said the chief inspector.

'I saw the umbrella come down the hill,' the boy said quickly. 'I got a good photo of that. You really will come, won't you?'

'I really will come,' said Morrissey, 'and I'm more than glad you want to help.' He put the receiver back with care and looked at Barrett. The sergeant was chewing rapidly, sensing his eating time was going to be less than he needed. Morrissey poured his cooling soup back into the flask and screwed the top in place. 'That was a very young photographer with pictures of the common taken about the time Gail Latimer was killed. He'd like us to see them,' he said.

Wanting to speak, Barrett tried to swallow too much and almost choked himself.

'Take your time,' Morrissey said kindly. He slapped vigorously at Barrett's back. 'You've got all of thirty seconds.'

As Barrett mopped his streaming eyes, he tried not to see the chief inspector's grin.

TWENTY-THREE

LOUISE HARDING heard about the latest murder from the girl behind the delicatessen counter at the supermarket, but she didn't learn who the victim had been until she listened to the lunch-time news. It shocked her. Murder was something that happened to people whom no one ever knew. She supposed most people comforted themselves with that thought. It wasn't true, of course, but it was one of those little subterfuges that made it possible to go on living. The alternative came in little bottles marked 'tranquillisers'.

Painfully she remembered the scene at Friday breakfast; Neville had been in a terrible rage, and for a while she had been afraid he would strike Mark. It wouldn't have been the first time, but a full-grown Mark was different from the boy he had been. She wondered if it was the knowledge that he was powerful enough to strike back that had kept the clenched fist from moving.

Damn it, she thought irritably, we live as though Neville has all the power. If he had, it was only because she'd been too weak and wrapped in self-misery to do anything about it. He hadn't seemed such a self-centred oaf when she married him.

But he wouldn't, would he? Whatever else Neville might be, he was no fool. He'd known just what he was doing being so nice; oh yes, so very nice to the boss's daughter. And afterwards there had been the children.

Irrational guilt for Natalie's death twitched at her. Mark had tried to deflect his father's anger from her, otherwise he wouldn't have said what he did say about Bill Thompson. She knew if it hadn't been for that, instead of coming home soon after eleven, her husband would have been with his mistress on Saturday night. And Natalie would still be alive. *Wouldn't she*?

THE HOUSE WAS almost exactly opposite the bus shelter on the common, and when Morrissey got out of the car a boy waved from an upstairs window. The chief inspector waved back.

It was obvious from her face that the woman who opened the door hadn't expected them. Morrissey showed his warrant card, and said, 'We'd like to have a chat with your son, Mrs Swift. He hasn't been up to anything, so don't worry about that, but we think he may have something that will help us.'

'Oh, heavens, and I was only out five minutes!' she said, and her forehead crumpled into wavy lines. 'He used the telephone and rang you, didn't he? I should have known he'd do that. After all the fuss he's made, I should have known.' She both looked and sounded upset, and Morrissey wondered what the source of it was.

During the house-to-house Mrs Swift had said that no one had seen anything from her home. For a second he wondered if the boy were a hoaxer, then he remembered that he couldn't have made up the black umbrella.

With an interrogative note, he said, 'No great crime though, is it, to ring the police?'

She hooked a strand of light auburn hair behind her ear, and Morrissey, guessing her age to be around thirty, saw that under her make-up she was smothered in freckles. What *was* she worried about? That the boy wasn't at school? A truanting problem, then.

She said, 'I don't seem to have any choice,' and moved back from the door. Barrett, last in, closed it, and she led them upstairs into a large front bedroom with luminous stars on the ceiling and pop star pin-ups on the walls.

If you discounted the two white mice, the hamster and a small aquarium, the boy was alone in his room. A boy with wide, intelligent grey eyes and red hair like his mother's, who shouldn't have been given a body so twisted that Morrissey wanted to cry out in sympathy.

'Well now, Colin Swift,' his mother said, 'you've done very well for yourself, a chief inspector, no less. I hope these photographs of yours warrant such importance.' It was exasperation that overlaid her voice, not anger, and hearing that, the boy's face cleared. He grinned and moved his wheelchair forward, shaking Morrissey's hand, and then Barrett's with a fragile grip. 'I'll put the kettle on,' she said, and left them alone.

Colin said, 'I have two jolly good cameras, do you want to see them?' He manoeuvred the chair behind a cabinet set at right angles to the window, the top cluttered with lenses, books and all the paraphernalia that went with his hobby. He said, 'This is a Hasselblad, it gets a very fine definition, but the one I use the most is this Pentax.' He grinned again. 'Of course it could be said that since it does everything but think, it's a bit of an idiot's camera. There's a film in; try it out, if you like. It's set up—you don't have to do anything but press the button.'

Morrissey took it and moved to the window, seeing the common miniaturised in the viewer. He found the copse of trees where Gail Latimer had died and his finger hovered over the button, then he moved the camera to an ice-cream van that had stopped near the corner and had a queue of children. The shutter clicked. He gave the camera back. 'Thank you. Will you let me know how it comes out?'

'I'll give you a print, of course. Will you fetch it, or shall I post it? I'd quite like it if you came again.'

'Then I'll do that,' said Morrissey. 'Now, what about these other photographs you have, the ones you rang me about?'

'They're in that brown envelope just behind you. Why don't you sit down for a bit; Mum's bringing some tea up. You can ask me about them, if you want.' The defensive hopefulness in his eyes made the chief inspector think that visitors were probably short on the ground.

Barrett said, 'We ca...' and got silenced by a look. Morrissey settled himself on a chair and opened the envelope. The prints were black and white and very clear, no fuzziness and no camera shake.

'I was using the tripod,' Colin said perceptively.

Morrissey nodded, looking at a black umbrella bowling down the hill, caught in mid-bounce. And Malcolm Livesey coming out of the bus shelter to retrieve it; another of him with it in his hand, standing looking up the common. 'Are they in order?' he said, and got a nod. He flicked through to the one before the umbrella; nothing. But the image before that was of the copse, and the one before that showed the umbrella again, tiny, being carried by someone and held out against the rain. He caught his breath.

'Was that her?' the boy said, sounding like Mike for ghoulish interest. 'What I really need, of course, is an enlarger, but Mum won't let me have one.'

'Why not?'

'Because he'll have to wait until Christmas,' his mother said, coming in with a tray. 'Santa Claus is too hard up the rest of the year.' She exchanged affectionate looks with her son. 'Been telling all your hard-luck stories?' she asked him.

'Yeah!' He scrunched his face into a caricature. 'Like how you don't feed me, and I got like this 'cos you kept me locked up in a suitcase. And now the cops know, you're for the hot seat, lady!' He looked at Morrissey and Barrett. 'I have some jolly good gangster films. Humphrey Bogart, James Cagney, George Raft; I think I might have liked the nineteen twenties. You can watch one, if you'd like.'

Morrissey, drinking his cup of tea quickly like Barrett, said honestly, 'I'd like to very much, but we haven't got the time. When I come back for the print, maybe.'

Colin looked delighted. 'I'll sort out the best one so it's ready.' He looked at the envelope in Morrissey's hand. 'Can I have those back when you've had a good look at them?'

'With grateful thanks from the CID,' said Morrissey, and stood up. 'I'll see you soon, Colin. You're a brilliant photographer.'

When they went downstairs, Colin's mother asked, 'Are they really going to be a help or were you humouring him?'

Morrissey looked at her. 'Is that why you didn't want him to talk to us, in case he got disappointed?'

She nodded. 'There isn't much in his life that hasn't disappointed him,' she pointed out.

'These,' he patted the envelope, 'could prove the biggest help yet.'

'Are they that good?' said Barrett as they got into the car.

The chief inspector waved up at the window. 'No,' he said. 'Better.'

TWENTY-FOUR

A PASSING patrol car had found Natalie Parkes's black Fiat parked in a lay-by near Brindley Woods, and when Morrissey got back to his office it had already been towed into the police garage. The forensic team were going to have a busy day with both that and Thompson's Montego. The lay-by was reasonably close to Bill Thompson's flat, which proved nothing, because only a fool would leave something incriminating on his own doorstep.

Colin Swift's prints and negatives had been sent to the photography lab with a request for maximum definition of the copse area, and now Morrissey badly wanted to talk to Neville Harding, but there was nothing to link him with the dead girl, except hearsay from Margaret. But Harding didn't know that.

Irritably he wondered why there was nothing on his desk from Smythe, and why the detective constable didn't seem to be in the building. He sent Barrett to find out.

Forensic reports had begun to come through, and he was uncomfortably conscious of the passage of time as he began to read through them. And then he knew that he was right, and Barrett was right: this killer had left clues, had been careless. Under the

dead woman's broken fingernails forensic had discovered traces of brown leather—no yellow rubber
gloves, this time. And under her right thumbnail, skin
cells that were not her own.

Morrissey felt a stir of optimism. The pubic comb-
out had provided blond hairs that were probably Bill
Thompson's, and the back of her dress revealed mi-
croscopic fragments of oiled wool from an Aran
sweater. There were other things, too: a dog had
fouled the grass behind the grave, and the print of a
rubber-soled trainer had been left in it, kept dry by
Natalie's body; on the ends of the knotted twine
traces of brown leather that matched that under her
fingernails; and from her tights, her dress, her hair,
her skin, fibres from a tartan travel rug.

Two lovers, one seemingly sure of her, the other
about to lose her. The urge to see Neville Harding
grew.

As he got up from his chair, Barrett came back with
excitement standing round him like an aura. He said,
'We've had a call about a man hanging around the
wharf who matches the photo-fit, and Smythe and
Inspector Beckett have gone out to pick him up.'

Morrissey stared at him and wondered if it could
really end so simply. He was waiting, with Barrett, in
the charge-room when they came back. The man with
them answered almost exactly the description Cedric
Stanley had given. The straggly hair and glasses were
the same, the heavy reek of tobacco, the roll-up machine in one pocket of the camouflage jacket. And a

mess of collected dog-ends in the others. Under the pale stubble of beard, he looked frightened. There was another reek from him, too: that of a long-unwashed body, and neither Katie nor Stanley had mentioned that.

Morrissey watched the wrinkling noses around him and wondered if they could have missed it. He looked at Beckett. 'Forensic first. Body swabs, cuts, scratches, and the clothes sent off.'

'And a bloody bath,' said Beckett, scratching at his thigh. 'When do you want to talk to him?'

'After the bath,' said Morrissey, as Smythe's free hand moved inside his jacket and copied Beckett's. 'No urgency, really; he's not going anywhere.'

BARRETT ARGUED, 'There can't be two men looking like that in Malminster; he must be the right one!'

'Must be, then?' said Morrissey, hoping Barrett was watching the bus in front that had just put its right indicator on. 'Leaving aside the fact that he has the shakes, they'd have smelled him coming from a mile off.'

'Could be camouflage.'

'Like the jacket,' said Morrissey. He braced himself as Barrett swung the car to the left and just got through the gap between bus and kerb. 'Altogether too new-looking to go with the rest of him; and if you saw anybody else drive like that, you'd be after them.'

'The shakes could be an act,' said Barrett as if he hadn't heard. 'And the smell—its easy enough to find places to pick up a smell if you want one bad enough. Take the pig farm up Stye Lane, for example. Downwind on a warm day, and there's not much difference between them and him.' He indicated, and turned left into the car park at the side of the newspaper building. 'What makes you think Harding is the mystery boyfriend?'

'When you get married,' said the chief inspector, 'you'll find that women have a wonderful and mysterious network for knowing exactly what's going on around them.'

'You mean the old biddies are gossiping, and Mrs Morrissey picked it up,' Barrett said with unthinking bluntness. 'I suppose it's like having unpaid snouts.' He turned off the engine and then, seeing Morrissey's face, started to back-track. 'Not that I'm suggesting Mrs Morrissey is part of that kind of set-up,' he blundered. 'Just that it's good she keeps her ears open.'

Morrissey got out and slammed the door, his long legs weaving between the parked cars, leaving Barrett to catch up. One spot, by the back entrance, was marked 'Editor.' A dark blue BMW was parked there. The chief inspector glanced inside as he passed and saw no tartan rug.

Morrissey had met Harding several times before, and found him a man to tolerate rather than like. That impression strengthened as they faced each other in the editor's office. Harding had a strong face, rawboned and flattish, pugnacious in the thrust of chin;

but the strength suggested bullish intent to have his way rather than reliability. And he didn't like having Morrissey in his office.

'You've got a nerve, pushing in here!' he said. 'What's the matter—did that editorial rattle you? Catch you with your leg up?'

Morrissey ignored the baiting. 'Did you see Natalie Parkes on Saturday night, after she left Bill Thompson?'

'I don't know what you're bloody talking about! Come to that, I don't think I want to. You're not my kind of policeman, Morrissey, barking up empty alleys. Go and catch your strangler instead of being petty.'

Barrett's undignified scuttle across the car park had left him disgruntled, and he had smoothed his hair, stroked the sparse gathering of hair on his top lip and tugged at his waistcoat while he listened. Now he forgot that and waited for Morrissey to lose his temper, writing fast in his notebook to catch up.

'Natalie Parkes,' Morrissey thundered. 'You set her up in a flat by the cricket field, paid her rent, got what you wanted in return. Don't bother to say you didn't—there are witnesses. You can't brush that sort of thing under the carpet, not with a girl like Natalie. Now I'll not ask again: Did you see her Saturday night?'

Like pit-bull terriers, they faced off across Harding's desk. 'You're too late,' Harding shouted. 'Too bloody late, as usual! I'd finished with the two-timing bitch. Spending my money and bedding Bill Thompson!'

'When?' Morrissey barked. 'Saturday night? You'd just found out, had you? Couldn't stand losing face, so you killed her.'

'I was home,' snapped Harding. 'Home at eleven. Get round that.'

'And what makes you think she wasn't killed before,' said Morrissey, suddenly silky quiet. 'To my best knowledge, nobody's said what time yet.'

'Not the point, is it?' said Harding. 'I'm saying when I got home, nothing else. And use your brains. There's that many courting couples down Honeypot Lane, it'd take a fool to chance it before midnight. And I'm no fool.'

'Natalie left Bill Thompson at nine o'clock to meet you,' Morrissey said. 'What happened when she did?'

'And who says that, then? Bill Thompson? He would, wouldn't he? What makes you think she left him at all? Suspended three months last year for blacking another player's eye in a temper. Forgotten that, had you? Maybe he lost it again with Natalie.'

'I'd like to see in the boot of your car,' said Morrissey. 'It's the BMW, is it? Parked outside. It won't take long.'

'I don't have to show you anything,' Harding said. 'But I will, because it'll make a damn good write-up for the weekend.' He came round the desk and out of the office without waiting for either of them, taking the stairs two at a time down to the back entrance.

The boot was big and roomy and would have held Natalie Parkes's body easily. Now it was empty. Barrett saw there was no travel rug there and felt almost let down, carried along by the chief inspector's seeming certainty. He'd been too expectant.

Harding slammed the lid and pocketed the keys. 'Seen enough?'

'Yes,' said Morrissey his face granite. 'That's a nasty scratch on your right wrist.'

'Rose bush.' Harding looking at it dismissively. 'Chief Inspector, I was in Bournemouth when the last girl died, and working here when the murder before that took place. Don't try to fit me in the bag, I'm too big and bulky.'

A car came into the car park and pulled into an empty space. Morrissey recognised the reporter from the cemetery, and saw the look of excitement.

Harding said, 'What's happened, Ken?'

'They've arrested somebody, haven't they? Or, at least,' he looked uneasily at Morrissey, 'they've got this odd-ball who matches the photo-fit, and from what I hear it's only a matter of time.'

Harding threw his head back and laughed out loud. 'Good god, Morrissey, you don't even know what's happening in your own backyard!'

And Morrissey, with his hands loose at his side, took a step closer to him, and said, 'Oh, I do, Mr Harding, better than you know. And I'd like you to come with me to answer questions at Malminster police station. You're not obliged to say anything, but...'

'You bloody idiot, get out of my way! I've work to do,' and Harding half-turned to go into the building, putting out a heavy-fisted arm to fend Morrissey off, and finding it held and pushed up behind his back.

'... anything you say may be taken down and used in evidence against you,' Morrissey finished, and pushed him towards the police car.

TWENTY-FIVE

OSGODBY SAID, 'For pity's sake, do you know who you've got down there? Have you charged him yet?'

'Not yet,' said Morrissey, getting ready to bite the bullet.

'If you're wrong, we'll be pilloried,' the chief superintendent moaned. 'That editorial last week was bad enough, but the next...' He shook his head. 'Everyone knows how the attack on Katie must have made you feel, but you clutch at a handful of straws and have them all guilty. First it was Appleby, then you've got a photo-fit look-alike in the cells, and now it's Harding. You're stretching my credulity, John, and I want you to sort it out before it gets to the CC.'

'It is sorted,' said Morrissey. 'I'm not making any claims that Harding killed the other three. What I am saying is that he killed Natalie Parkes.'

'I hope you've got proof of that?'

'I will have,' said Morrissey. 'Given time.' He smiled bleakly. 'And a search warrant.' He saw Osgodby's head begin to shake, and said, 'There has to be a search warrant. We can't hold back just because he is who he is and it might be difficult.'

'Damn it, John, why didn't you say before that you thought the Parkes girl's death wasn't linked to the others? You leave me out on a limb; I've just got back from County Headquarters, and you drop this on me. Just like that, with no warning! And all you've got is a bit of gossip, a scratch he says came from a rose bush, and him giving an alibi before you asked for one. And you're going to hang him on that?'

'I hope I am,' said Morrissey.

But there was always the chance that, even if he were right, it would be more difficult than that. The sweater and rug could have been washed, the trainers cleaned. They could have been given to a local charity shop or dumped on a tip. He wondered if, knowing about her husband's affair, Louise Harding would still want to help him if he were guilty? Where loyalty was concerned, women remained a mystery to the chief inspector. He didn't know why they went back time after time to a man who would beat them again, or waited most of their lives for men who were back in jail almost before they had time to say hello.

Osgodby's worry showed. If things went wrong, it wouldn't only be Morrissey who had to pay. He sucked on his teeth. 'It had better come good this time, John. I suppose it's another ninety per cent hunch and ten per cent logic like last time?'

Morrissey smiled again, knowing the chief superintendent referred to the Little Henge murders. That time, a hunch *had* paid off.

Osgodby remembered that, too, and looked discomfited. 'I'll not hold you back, then,' he said, and Morrissey nodded and left him to worry alone.

Downstairs, Harding's solicitor was creating a rumpus, his manner as bellicose as that of his client. When he saw Morrissey, he exploded, 'A man of Neville Harding's character in the cells! You're going to find yourself in serious trouble, this time; there are such things as disciplinary committees, you know. I want my client out and free, or I get a habeas corpus.'

'You can try,' said the chief inspector, 'but you know it wouldn't work. We have a right to hold anyone for questioning—even you, if the evidence warranted it.'

'Is that a threat?'

'No, it's a statement of fact,' said Morrissey, and stepped round him, leaving the problem for someone else. Behind him, he heard the solicitor say, 'I shall go to the Chief Constable,' and winced inwardly with the knowledge that Osgodby would be the first to have his ear burned.

THE HARDINGS LIVED on the east side of Malminster, where the town gave way to open country. It was an old house, double fronted, with a porticoed entrance that gave it a look of self-importance, and Morrissey's first thought was that it would cost a fortune to heat. The gravel drive sloped down from house to road and circled an island of shrubs, mostly laurel and rhododendron. Barrett had driven along it gently, hearing pebbles leap to hit the underside of the car.

'You'd think he'd have it tarmacked,' he complained when they stopped. Morrissey, knowing Barrett's usual speeding approach, just raised his eyebrows. Barrett looked up at the house. 'Think we should have brought some help?' he said. 'Must be six or seven bedrooms, by the look of it.'

'Let's see how it goes,' said Morrissey. 'We can always radio back.'

He expected a maid or a housekeeper, but instead it was Louise Harding herself who came to the door. She let them in without a quibble and he wondered why she didn't look surprised to see them. Then she told him.

'Neville's solicitor has been in touch,' she said. 'It's about the death of Natalie Parkes, isn't it?'

Harding's wife wore two-inch heels and her head still barely came to the chief inspector's shoulder, which meant she had to tilt her head to look at him. She must once have had a good figure but now it was thickening, and there was a heavy sprinkling of grey in the mid-brown hair that she didn't trouble to hide. He saw that, unlike many women of her age who turned to heavier make-up, hers remained discreet, and the lines etched on her face told him that life had had its problems.

There was no easy way for Morrissey to say what he had to say, and so he was blunt. 'Did you know that your husband was involved with Miss Parkes?' He waited to see if dismay or anger came first, but he got neither.

Without hesitation, she said, 'Of course. It's been going on for over a year; nothing could remain a secret for that length of time. Certainly not in Malminster, if it involved a man like Neville and concerned sinful sex.' There was irony in her voice. 'There are worse things happening, and people don't turn a hair about them. It was Neville's disloyalty that bothered me where Natalie was concerned, not the sex part, although it shouldn't have surprised me.' She squinted up at him, and asked, 'Can you imagine the fall of man being caused by such a furiously funny act?'

'No,' said Morrissey, relieved that there were going to be no tears and no denials. 'I can't. Do you know where your husband was on Saturday?'

'Playing golf, most of the day. Then he went out in the evening and came home about eleven.'

'Do you remember what he was wearing?'

'When? For golf, or later? Let's see. He has a pair of checked slacks in bright blue, he was wearing those for golf, with a blue shirt and a yellow Pringle sweater. And later he changed into a dark grey suit and white shirt. Is that what you wanted?'

'Not an Aran sweater?'

'He doesn't have one. Or at least I haven't seen him wear one. Perhaps he kept some clothes at Natalie's flat that I don't know about. I suppose he might have wanted a younger image there.'

'Do you know where he went on Saturday night?'

'That isn't something I ever bothered asking. And, if I had, Neville wouldn't have told me.'

'You're being very honest.'

'I wouldn't have been, a few days ago, but I've been reassessing things since yesterday, and I realise there are a lot of things I ought to have faced up to before, instead of pretending they weren't there. Things like that are very difficult for women of my generation. Now I'm being honest with myself.' She looked at the folded paper he had taken from his pocket. 'Is that a search warrant?'

'Yes,' said Morrissey. 'I'm sorry.'

'Where to you want to start?'

'Where your husband's clothes are kept.'

'It's the second room on the right; mine is next to it, and my son Mark is on the other side. The other three rooms are empty now that my two older children live away from home.'

Barrett moved towards the stairs, and Louise Harding asked, 'I'll put the kettle on, shall I? We might as well be civilised.' She went away to the back of the hall, and into the kitchen.

Barrett said, 'I didn't think she'd be that calm. Think it's shock? I mean finding her husband's been locked up because his girlfriend's been murdered would have most women swinging off the ceiling!'

'You've got a terribly poor opinion of women,' said Morrissey. 'You'd better watch yourself or they might find out, and much good that'd do your reputation!

How are you making out with Janet Yarby these days? Still not interested, isn't she?'

Mention of the WPC had always been a sore point; the more Barrett tried, the more discouraging the young policewoman became. Morrissey looked back over his shoulder, satisfied when he saw the sergeant was glowering.

There was no Aran sweater in Harding's bedroom, but there were three pairs of trainers, all of which were fairly new and none of them with caked treads. They moved to his wife's bedroom and found only her possessions, while the third bedroom, where her son slept, looked remarkably like Mike's with its posters and hi-fi system. But there were line drawings and unframed paintings, too, and even Morrissey's untutored eye could tell they were good. He remembered that, like Katie, Harding's son went to art college.

It was Barrett, turning out the dirty-linen basket in the bathroom, who found the sweater, and when they took it downstairs and showed it to Louise Harding, she shook her head dismissively, and said, 'Oh no, that isn't Neville's, it belongs to Mark. I knitted it myself.'

Barrett, stuffing it into a plastic bag, said, 'Did your son know Natalie Parkes, too? Was he upset that his father was carrying on?'

'No.'

'No, he didn't know, or no, he wasn't upset?'

'Yes, he knew; no, he wasn't upset. Why should he be? He's never had reason to think his father was a paragon.'

'But he might not have liked its effect on you.'

She said, 'That's ridiculous,' but she looked worried.

Morrissey said, 'Was your son at home on Saturday night?'

She shook her head. 'No, he went to the Saturday night student disco. He came home on the back of Peter Heslop's motorbike about one.' She rubbed her hands as though they were suddenly cold, and said, 'I'll make some tea.'

Morrissey shook his head. 'Another time, perhaps. Does your husband usually carry a travelling rug in his car?'

'I don't think so. There's an old one in the hall cupboard that we used for picnics years ago, but it's larger than a travelling rug.' She went out into the hall and opened a door beneath the stairs, switching on the light so that she could see. As she reached to pull down a blanket from the shelf, Barrett bent and picked up a pair of muddy-soled trainers, and Harding's wife hugged the blanket in her arms and said they were Mark's, too.

TWENTY-SIX

THERE WAS A NEED for the man brought in from the wharves to be interviewed, and Inspector Beckett had agreed to do that, with Barrett unwillingly coerced into sharing the chore. Morrissey had argued that since the detective sergeant was so familiar with the case, he should be there, ready to pick up any pieces that fitted into the puzzle as he knew it. Accepting the idea without enthusiasm, Barrett wondered pessimistically if it was less his knowledge and more his absence that motivated Morrissey's mind.

It was late afternoon when Morrissey drove into the art college car park. Classes had ended at four-thirty, but Mark Harding had stayed behind as he often did, working in the quiet of the studio to build up a portfolio of work. A handful of other students were similarly occupied, surprised to be interrupted by Morrissey. The chief inspector had deliberately decided to talk to Mark alone, letting his instinct act as guide. One day, he supposed, he would be wrong and the sky would fall on his head. But not today; hearing the speech impediment that plagued Harding's son, he felt glad not to have Barrett there; another face would have only added to the pressure.

On that floor of the building, all the tutors' offices were locked, making the only available place to talk a smaller studio where no one seemed to be working. Morrissey looked inquisitively at the long tables and heavy frames, the bright pots of colour stacked on shelves.

'Sc-Sc-Scrimp-Scrimp...' Eyes closed and mouth working, Mark forced out the right words, 'Scr-reen printing.' He moved his arms out expansively, embracing the room, and Morrissey cursed himself for not having asked Louise Harding more about her son. Was it only a speech impediment, or was it more? A dark-haired girl, plump and pretty, wandered in and came to them, putting her arm round Mark and hugging him as she might a younger brother. But Mark wasn't younger, although the smile he gave her had that kind of innocence in it.

She said, 'Managing, or shall I stay?'

'We're doing fine,' Morrissey said firmly. 'And it has to be just Mark and me.'

'That's because you're fuzz.' She upped her eyebrows and thumped Mark playfully. 'Nicking kids' lollies again! Told you you'd get caught one day, didn't I?'

'Not m-m-me!'

She grinned, and bounced away from them. As she went out, Mark said, 'C-laire,' and rolled his eyes.

'Looks after you, does she?' said Morrissey. 'Nice girl. My daughter is an art student.' Mark registered surprise. The chief inspector said, 'Katie Morrissey; she knows you.'

'P-retty, bu-t, bu-t, b-ossy.' Mark raised his hand and brought his fingers and thumb together, opening and closing them like a mouth, and Morrissey's face twitched, recognising Katie's talent for talking.

The chief inspector said, 'I've been speaking to your mother—she said she knitted you an Aran sweater, a nice one, I've seen it. When did you wear it last?'

His forehead creased, Mark shook his head and said finally, 'Twicks.'

Morrissey said, 'Two weeks?' and got a look of relief. He went on, 'There was a pair of Adidas trainers in the hall cupboard that were yours, too; well worn, comfortable looking.'

'T-oo-oo sm-all.' Mark leaned back on the table behind him and lifted both feet from the ground. The canvas baseball boots were at least size nine, with the Converse All-Star logo over each ankle. But feet could be crammed into smaller shoes if it had to be done for a purpose.

Morrissey said in the same easy voice, 'Did you know Natalie Parkes?' and the boy's face flushed deep red. His mouth moved wordlessly. Morrissey sighed, recognising how slow the process could be. Chances were, the more Mark felt harassed, the harder it would be for him to talk. He said, 'I think you should go home now. Why not put your things away? I'll give you a lift.'

Without argument, Mark went back into the bigger room and began to pack away his things.

Claire put down her pencil and came to them. 'He isn't really in trouble, is he?' she asked, and scowled, looking as though she would rush to Mark's defence if he were threatened. Around them the other students stopped work to watch, and only Mark himself seemed unconcerned.

'Nicking lollies is always a serious offence!' said Morrissey. 'But, as it happens, I'm giving Mark a lift home. Did you go to the disco on Saturday?'

'Would I miss it?' She lifted her arms and did a couple of gyrations. 'Everybody goes. Well…almost.'

He said, 'How about you, Mark. Were you there?'

Mark nodded. Claire said, 'Lucky sod got a ride home on Pete's new Kawasaki. Some people have it made!'

'What time was that? After the disco ended?'

'Mm. Half-twelvish. My turn next week.'

'R-Ready,' said Mark, zipping his canvas holdall, and with a chorus of mock police sirens behind them he and Morrissey went out of the studio and down the stairs.

Louise Harding looked first surprised and then half afraid when she saw the chief inspector with her son, and Morrissey waited until Mark was upstairs and out of earshot before asking if the speech impediment were just that.

A loud swell of pop music flowed downstairs and then quietened a little. She told him of her fall downstairs and the oxygen starvation it had caused her son.

Morrissey sensed continuing guilt, and wished he didn't have to add to it. He said, 'Did Mark know the full extent of his father's relationship with Natalie Parkes?'

She took in a deep breath and looked down at the carpet. The silence stretched. Then she seemed to make up her mind and told him about the Friday morning upset. 'I think that was the reason Neville broke off the affair with her,' she said. 'He would hate to know Natalie had someone else; he's very jealous of his possessions.'

If that were the first Neville Harding had heard of Bill Thompson, it would have incensed him. Probably enough for the idea of murder to enter his mind. And if Natalie had admitted it on Saturday, told him it was over, the final impetus would be there. A man like Harding wouldn't accept being discarded. But he must have almost decided before he met her; planned to be clever and make it look like one more victim for the man he had called a cowardly attacker. *But he hadn't known to plait the twine.*

Morrissey said, 'I haven't told Mark about his father. Will you be able to do it?'

'Fred Burridge said it was all a mistake.'

But Harding's solicitor didn't know all the facts. The chief inspector said, 'Tell him, anyhow. It's only fair, and it's better for you to tell him than hear it from someone else.'

Louise Harding said, 'But he didn't know the other three girls. In fact, he wasn't even here when the second one died; he'd gone down to Wapping for an editors' meeting. One of those "let the provincials have a sniff of the big time" things.'

Morrissey said, 'We're not really looking for that kind of connection.'

Understanding came. 'Thank you,' she said, 'for bringing Mark home.'

IT WAS SIX-THIRTY, and Morrissey knew the day was passing too fast. He'd learned a lot, but there was still more to do. He didn't know whether or not to be glad that Tim Beal was waiting for him.

'I thought I'd better come when Mum told me you'd been round,' said Tim. 'I mean, I didn't know about it until I got back today.' There was an almost haggard look about him, and Morrissey remembered the unrequited crush on his daughter. 'I passed Katie half-way down the Drive. If I'd given her a lift the rest of the way...I thought about it, you know; I thought about it, and then I thought— What the heck, she won't go out with me, let her walk.' He hung his head. 'It was bloody stupid!'

'You weren't to know she was in any danger,' said Morrissey. 'Did you see anybody behind her?'

'No, but I thought I saw someone turn into one of the houses. I suppose that was him keeping out of the headlights.'

'It probably was,' said the chief inspector. 'No idea at all what he looked like?'

'Just a shadow,' said Tim. 'Can I go and see Katie?'

'I don't see why not; she's getting better now. Probably be glad of a visitor.' He couldn't think what it was about Tim that made the chemistry fail to work. Personally Morrissey rather liked him. Perhaps that was it; he was too acceptable.

Margaret's parents hadn't liked her going out with a policeman. He wondered belatedly if that had been part of his attraction for her. Too late now to worry. Then he remembered his own instinctive bristling when he saw Hicks in Katie's room.

He went downstairs, looking for Beckett, and tried to analyse what made Tim a better prospect for his daughter than a young PC. The answer evaded him. Inspector Beckett was in the canteen, an empty plate in front of him, a half-drunk mug of coffee on the table. Barrett was with him.

'Bloody waste of time, that was!' said Beckett when he saw Morrissey. 'Spaced out of his tiny skull. You know them bloody glasses? Can't see out of 'em, can he? Says some bugger left 'em there while he was asleep; clothes as well.' He narrowed his eyes at Morrissey's lack of response. 'You knew, didn't you?'

'I thought it was likely,' the chief inspector admitted, sitting down and giving Barrett's empty mug a push. He said, 'If you're fetching another, you can bring me one. Weak!' he bellowed after Barrett.

'Turns out he's schizophrenic let out on this bloody community care scheme,' Beckett said. 'Can you credit it? Sleeping rough down Calder Wharf for weeks. An' he's run out of medication.' Glumly he watched Barrett coming back. 'He's still here, waiting for his social worker to come and sort him out.'

Morrissey said, 'Well, we know one thing. The clothes weren't left there by accident; we were meant to pick them up.'

'I'd worked that out for myself,' said Beckett. 'Right bloody joker we're after!'

'Except that now we know he goes past the wharf often enough to know—what do they call him?'

'Billy Rush.'

'To know Rush was there,' said Morrissey. 'He's starting to make mistakes.'

Barrett said, 'Down the wharf and up Calder Street, and you come out across from the park where Susan Howarth died.'

Beckett sat up. 'Worth a watch, do you reckon?' he asked Morrissey.

'It's an option,' the chief inspector admitted, 'but a lot of people use that short cut.' He wrapped his hands round the mug in front of him and stared into the darkling brew. Harding was guilty he had no doubts there, and now he sensed he was drawing close to the other man too. 'Have those blow-ups come yet?' he asked Barrett.

'On your desk about an hour ago.' He watched Morrissey take a gulp of coffee and screw up his face. 'I did ask for it weak,' he said.

Beckett reached out. 'Give it here,' he said. 'I've been wanting to have a go at somebody.' He took the mug back to the counter and barked. 'Come here, Charlie! Look at this bloody pot! You can't call that weak, it'd kill a pigeon!' Charlie, who was fat and perspiring, didn't quibble. Beckett came back with a fresh mug. 'Spineless,' he complained. 'Didn't even answer back.' His bleeper went, and his face took on a wolfish look. 'That'll be Billy's social worker,' he said. 'I'll go and have words.'

TWENTY-SEVEN

MIKE SHOULD HAVE been home by five, but it was nearly six when he came, using his front-door key instead of coming in through the kitchen, and going straight upstairs. Margaret had been waiting for him, at first impatient because they were going to visit Katie, and then feeling worry start to edge in. When she heard the front door slam and his feet on the stairs, and he hadn't even called out to her, anger came. He'd been moody ever since the attack on Katie, spending most of his time upstairs.

Until now, she had put it down to shock. But to be deliberately late when he knew she was waiting for him and that Katie would wonder why they hadn't come... Well, that was a different thing altogether, and it was time she sorted a few things out with her son.

Annoyed and upset, she found he was in the bathroom with the door locked, and aimlessly straightened things that were in no need of it as she waited for the sound of the cistern. When it didn't come, she knocked on the bathroom door.

There was a grunt.

'Mike, if you're not on the loo, come and open the door.'

'Go 'way.' In its thickness the voice didn't sound like Mike, and worry touched her again. When the children were small, Morrissey had fitted a safety bolt to the bathroom door and its screw went through to the outside, flat and large enough for a coin to fit in the groove and turn it. Until now, the precaution had been unnecessary. With a feeling of guilt, she got a twopenny piece and heard the bolt click back.

Mike's bloody face was bent over the basin, and the flannel in his hand was red.

HARDING REMAINED outwardly bullish, but there was uneasiness, too. He'd refused to give a skin scraping from his wrist. The forensic officer had put the unused glass slide back in its box, remembering the mountain of work already waiting, and not prepared to waste sweat over one more test.

But then, brisk, in a manner making it more a matter of information than anything else, he'd said, 'I don't suppose anybody pointed out that skin cells aren't all that hard to come by? A pair of underpants from the wash-basket, and we've got you typed, anyway.'

The thin, wiry man who had seen Natalie Parkes's body in the cemetery derived a certain satisfaction from having pierced the editor's arrogance, and Harding had known it. What he hadn't known about until then, still wasn't sure about, was the possibility that skin cells could be matched with the amount of accuracy that was being suggested. Beyond any possibility of error?

That was a worry.

He'd expected Burridge to have pulled strings and oiled the right wheels to have had him out well before he had to face Morrissey again. It hadn't happened, however, and he made no effort to disguise his antagonism when he was taken to an interview room, his eyes going with hostile dislike from the chief inspector to Barrett, and from him to the tape-recorder.

'I'm saying nothing until you get Fred Burridge here,' he said. 'So you can either get him back or waste your time. But I'll tell you something: I wouldn't fancy being in your shoes when I get out of this place!'

Morrissey ignored the threat; Harding was where he wanted him to be, and that was the important thing. And Burridge had already been told. He said so to Harding, remembering the unmistakable gloom that had come across in the solicitor's tone and guessing it stemmed from his client's indiscriminate abuse. The rules of the game were: don't shoot your friends, but Harding didn't seem to recognise that.

'We could get a few things sorted out while we wait,' the chief inspector said. 'Such as why you refused a skin scrape. I'd expect an intelligent man like yourself, with a reasonable knowledge of modern police methods, to realise that type of test can as easily prove innocence as guilt.'

'Oh, yes? Well, I recognise it, all right, and I recognise something else as well,' said Harding. 'It could let you fit me up. I've told you you'll get nothing, not a damn thing. If you want to know what I've got to say, wait until you read the paper on Friday.'

'Thinking about that, let's look at a few facts. Did you know that statistically around eighty per cent of murder victims know their killer, and out of those, a high percentage die at the hands of their spouse or lover? Interesting, don't you think?'

'Not very. You're looking for a serial killer, Morrissey. Get on with it, and leave poor bloody innocents alone.'

'Is that how you see yourself, a poor bloody innocent? Let me tell you a story about a man who couldn't stand being dropped for someone younger and probably a damn sight better in bed. He thought he'd kill her cleverly, make it look like another serial murder, but he didn't know enough about it. And although he wore gloves, we know she scratched him with her thumbnail because his skin was still underneath it at post-mortem. He wore a pair of trainers that left a perfect sole-print, and an Aran sweater that left fibres on her clothing. And then he crammed her in the boot of a car and left her there for at least an hour, probably more, before he dumped her in the cemetery.'

'I don't wear trainers, and I don't wear Aran sweaters,' Harding said tersely.

'You must wear trainers sometimes,' Morrissey pointed out. 'There were three pairs in your wardrobe.'

'Try matching them.'

'We have.'

'And?'

'The soles were clean, and the treads didn't match.' The chief inspector leaned on the table. 'But the man in the story had a son, and the son's trainers were soiled with dog-dirt, and the pattern did match. Not only that, but this man's wife had knitted her son an Aran sweater, and it was in the wash-basket. I've no doubt forensic will find traces of Natalie Parkes on it.'

'Maybe she'd had a fancy for him, too.'

'What kind of man, Mr Harding, would wear his son's clothes to commit murder in?'

Harding shifted, met Morrissey's eye, shifted again and looked away. 'What kind of policeman,' he said, 'would think he had?'

'I would,' said Morrissey with grim certainty. 'I would.'

BURRIDGE HAD BEEN out of breath, and Morrissey had nodded at Barrett to close the tape, saying apologetically, 'We've decided there isn't any purpose to be served by interviewing Mr Harding any further at this time; sorry you've had a wasted journey.' He stared at Harding's glowering face, less healthily ruddy now, like that of a man who has eaten the wrong food, and said, wolf-kindly, 'You can have a

chat with him, if you like, see if there's anything else
he wants to tell you.' And then with Barrett he went
out of the room and left them to it.

In the upstairs corridor, on a chair outside Morrissey's office door, Hicks was waiting. Thoughts of
Katie pushed other things from the chief inspector's
mind. Barrett, with the office door closed on him,
went to put his feet up in the CID room and think on
what he'd been listening to downstairs. It was a neat
scenario that Morrissey had painted, and contempt
for Harding grew apace. For once, he didn't give any
thought to his chief being wrong.

Hicks, stiffly at attention even though he was sitting down, said, 'It probably isn't relevant, sir, but I
attended a domestic disturbance the week after
Christmas at the house where Diane Anderson lived.'

Morrissey leaned forward across his desk. 'Then
why the hell haven't you said so before?' he demanded. 'It's not up to you to decide relevance.' Then
he repented. 'Go ahead. Let's hear the rest of it.'

Hicks said, 'An old terrace house turned into flats,
three floors and the basement. There was a couple
living in the second floor back, not married, and the
woman had been left with a black eye and a cut lip.
The cohabitee had run off before I arrived, and she
didn't want to press charges.'

'Diane?' said Morrissey sharply.

'No, sir, Mandy Walters, but she was going to
spend the rest of the night in a neighbour's flat, and
I'm sure she used the name Diane. I got the impres-

sion it was the neighbour who'd rung up when she heard the rumpus. I checked on what to do, and got told to leave it if Mandy Walters wasn't willing to go to court. And she wasn't.'

'Did you go back?'

'No, sir.' He looked uneasy. 'I would have thought about it before, sir, but when Diane Anderson was killed I was on an instruction course, and I only found out where she lived today, when I saw the address on a file sheet in the computer room.'

Morrissey said, 'Then I'll commend instead of hanging you! How was Katie when you left?'

Hicks said pinkly, 'A bit better, I think, sir,' and Morrissey frowned, remembering the chess game. He hoped that was all Hicks had been playing at. Hicks said, 'She was a bit worried because her mother was late, I said she'd probably got held up in traffic.'

But Margaret should have been there, and Mike too.

The chief inspector said, 'What time was that?' and when Hicks said half-past six, felt his neglected stomach send out an anxious spurt of acid.

TWENTY-EIGHT

THE WARD SISTER'S voice was faintly Irish in Morrissey's ear, and too cheerful by far. He had tried his home first, and when the telephone went unanswered, been sure that by then his wife and son would be with Katie. Now this woman was telling him it wasn't so.

'Have you lost her, then? And you a policeman, too,' she said, as if he'd set Margaret down somewhere and then forgotten where. 'If you want to hold on a minute, I've got a message for you somewhere.' There was a rustle of papers and a faint clatter before she came back. 'Mrs Morrissey's in Casualty and I'm to tell you not to worry. Mike has a cut on his head and needs a couple of stitches.'

Only when he'd thanked her and hung up did new worry start about his son.

Barrett, seeing the initial relief, let himself relax. He said, 'It's all right, then? She's there?'

Morrissey frowned. 'But not with Katie. Mike's in Casualty needing stitches in his head, and don't ask me why, because I don't know.' He reasoned with himself why his son should be hurt. A scrum gone wrong at rugger practice? In front of him, spread out on his desk, were blow-ups of the copse area on the common, enlarged from the negatives Colin Swift had given them. On the original prints it had been obvious, from his choice of filter, that the boy's chief interest that day had been the swelling, drooping cloud formations. It was sheer luck that on one exposure he'd caught Gail Latimer at the top of the rise, walking down past the copse, every crease and curve of cloud behind her clearly defined. Then, uninterested in one more female crossing the common, he'd swung away and caught a fork of lightning. Luck again, obviously: it was impossible to predict accurately when the flash would come. And then something else again had caught his eye and he'd gone back to the path. When he did, the umbrella had already started its journey down the hill.

Morrissey went back to the image of Gail Latimer. The umbrella was held at an angle in front of her, her face almost hidden by it, the little that he could see turned sideways towards the copse.

Barrett, looking over his shoulder, said, 'It looks like she'd heard something, or seen something, but I still can't see what.' And then they both saw the same thing; the pale patch of a hand on the trunk of a birch; not on the edge of the copse, but further in, where it was deeply shadowed. It could have been just a bigger patch of silver, except that the fingers were spread. 'Rubber gloves,' said Barrett. 'I bet he had 'em on. One more frame in the same place, and we'd have got him.'

'I think,' said Morrissey, drawing a pencil circle, 'that's a bit of his head—dark hair, probably, from the look of it—and if it is his head, it's going to tell us how tall he is. Might not be much, but it's more than we've got now.'

He set it aside. It was the last view of the copse, and the remaining photographs had been enlarged in their entirety. The umbrella, bowling downhill, surreal in its isolation; the man coming from the bus shelter; the beginning of his movement up the hill, and then his girlfriend calling him back. The last exposure was of them together, heads close under the umbrella. After that, Colin had gone back to the skyline.

Morrissey flicked through the remaining exposures as quickly as he had in Colin's room, and saw one he'd overlooked before.

Because of the angle, the boy had captured the road, too. There was a car coming towards the camera, but that didn't attract the chief inspector's attention; what did was the white van that had stopped across the road. Under the black umbrella, the couple were buying ice-cream. A small excitement stirred. If the van had passed the top of the common and the crescent of houses where Appleby lived, its driver could have seen a man, walking, running, or driving, and not known the importance of what he saw.

He began to clear his desk, thinking that it was always the same; one day nothing, the next too many strings to follow and all needing to be picked up at the same time. He would let Barrett deal with the domestic dispute.

He said, 'Something that needs doing, Neil,' and passed on Hicks's report about the warring couple. There was only a slim chance it had anything to do with their murder enquiry, but if Diane Anderson was involved, they needed to know what happened next. He suggested, 'It's late, and you might not get anywhere until morning, but give it a try... And get Smythe to see if the photo lab can coax up a bigger and better image of that birch.' He gathered up his briefcase.

'Going home?' Barrett enquired politely.

Morrissey said severely, 'I'm going to make sure Harding's son didn't stop off anywhere when he got a lift home on Saturday night,' and went out of the office.

Barrett watched him go. It was all right for Morrissey, he had a wife to go home to. Glumly he thought of Michelle, and wondered if he'd ever get to finish what he'd started.

On his way downstairs, he met WPC Janet Yarby coming up. She gave him an encouraging smile. 'I hear you're doing well on this one, Neil,' she said.

The hint of warm approval was so totally unexpected that for once he was lost for words, and all he could do was grin foolishly at her shapely legs as she went into Inspector Beckett's office.

MARGARET WAS still in Casualty, and Mike had been X-rayed. Now his head was being stitched, and he was in one of the cubicles. When Morrissey heard that his son had been mugged walking through the underpass, his anger rose. There had been half a dozen incidents around there over the last two months, but Mike was the first to be injured. Because he put up more of a fight, or because he was Morrissey's son?

The thought came to the chief inspector that he was becoming paranoid. And the muggers were teenage, probably school-leavers, probably unemployed. They knew that much from witnesses, and from the times of day handbags had been snatched. Until Mike, the victims had been women over fifty who were easy targets. Harding's newspaper had called the thugs 'Granny Grabbers'. He wondered what would happen when the alienated young finally took over the world: Armageddon?

'They were disturbed,' Margaret said unsteadily, 'or it would have been worse.' She tried to smile. 'At least we seem to be getting all the bad things over with at one fell swoop. Will you call in on Katie? Because, if you do, tell her we're coming better late than never. Mike wants to see her, but I shan't let him stay long.' Hope flickered. 'Are you finished? Will you be coming home with us?'

Morrissey shook his head, wishing he could tell her yes, since it was what she so obviously wanted. 'I'm hoping to be home around ten,' he said. 'Tell Mike I came.' He squeezed her hand and went out through the swing doors.

He had expected Katie to be alone, but Hicks, changed into jeans and sweatshirt, was back playing chess, and there was a fresh vase of daffodils and irises on the bed-table. Morrissey glowered, and Hicks grew pink again as he stood up.

Katie's croak was still painful to hear. 'Ian brought flowers. Aren't they nice?'

She looked pleased and happy, and her father realised with a slight shock that these were the first flowers she had been given. Boyfriends she'd had in plenty, but none of them had paid her tribute in this way.

Did Hicks fancy his chances, then? There were things he would say to the young constable, but not in front of his daughter.

'Very nice,' he said, stonily advancing to Katie's bed. He rumpled her hair and got a disapproving squint. 'Mum's on her way,' he said. 'Mike got himself into a bit of a scuffle and needed some stitches.' Katie looked suddenly scared. 'Only kids messing about,' her father said quickly, knowing her mind had leapt to her own attacker. 'Nothing else.'

She relaxed. 'Poor Mike! Go get 'em.'

'I intend to,' said Morrissey looking at Hicks. 'Can I give you a lift?' he suggested pointedly.

'I drove here, but thank you very much, sir,' Hicks said politely.

Defeated, Morrissey planted an awkward fatherly kiss on his daughter's cheek, and left.

IN THE Cock and Crown in Victoria Street, most of the drinkers ignored the flickering TV, but those who watched the ten o'clock news bulletin heard that a man answering the photo-fit description was helping with police enquiries.

A feeling of largesse came over the sharp-faced man drinking at the bar, and he paid for an extra round of drinks. 'Celebrating,' he said, when he got funny looks. 'They've caught him, haven't they? Got him locked up. Worth a couple of pints, that.'

And they believed him.

The feeling of having put one over on Morrissey again was good. He could do nothing wrong, and thinking about the down-and-out who'd slept rough on the wharf, he reckoned to have done him a favour. There'd be at least a couple of nights' free board and lodging out of it.

Laughing at his own genius, he wet himself and went to empty his bladder, drying off the damp patch under the hand-dryer before he went back. He knew he would kill again very soon, and let his mind dwell on the girl he had lived with before Diane interfered. The remembered pleasure of violence roused him, and he opened his fly and went back into the cubicle.

While he was gone, the landlord set down four bitters and a black and tan, and said, 'He's getting

worse, you know. Bloody half-loaded, if you ask me.
I mean, he's not right, is he? Not a full pack.' When
no one took him up on it, he moved down to the other
end of the bar and watched the darts match instead.

TWENTY-NINE

PETER HESLOP told Morrissey, 'No, we didn't stop anywhere. I wanted to get a take-away, but Mark said he'd rustle up something at his place.'

'And did he?'

'Yep. Vegeburger and fried egg butties. Not bad. You should try them some time; at least you won't get BSE.'

'Mrs Harding cook them for you, did she?'

'No. Mark.'

'But she was there?' Morrissey queried. 'Waiting up, perhaps?'

'She came down in her dressing-gown to say his dad was home and don't make too much noise, and went back to bed. We were pissed off having to keep the ghettoblaster down; you need the decibels to get the right feel.' He shrugged. 'Waste, as well, since his old man wasn't there.'

'What makes you say that?' asked Morrissey, wondering if this would be the evidence he needed to push Harding into a corner.

Peter pushed up his left sleeve and showed Morrissey a wide, sore, friction burn. 'And the bike's dented,' he complained. 'I came off at Topliss's farm, thanks to old man Harding. If I hadn't gone in the ditch, I'd have hit him.'

'How do you know it was Harding?' said Morrissey.

'Because I recognised the BMW; there's not many that size in Malminster. It would be hard to mistake it for anything else.'

'He didn't stop when you came off?'

'No, but he must have known what happened. I suppose with his old lady thinking he was in bed, it wouldn't have been blamed on him anyway, would it? I was lucky I'd slowed right down for the corner. It's a new bike, and I wasn't taking chances.'

But Harding had been, the chief inspector thought. He said, 'Would you be prepared to put what you've just told me into a statement form?'

'And drop Mark's dad in it?' Peter Heslop looked wary. 'I don't know...I like Mark, and his dad's hard enough to live with, as it is.'

'It isn't the motoring offence; it's the time you saw him that matters. What time would it be? Half-past one?'

'Nearer two, maybe a bit after. I left Mark's house just after ten to. How will it affect him if I make a statement?'

'It won't do him any personal harm,' Morrissey promised.

'All right, then,' said Peter. 'When?'

'Tomorrow morning. Early as you like.'

'Before classes, then,' Peter said. 'I'll put the alarm on. I'm not that good at waking up.'

LATE AS IT WAS, Morrissey had wanted to talk to Malcolm Livesey and Lorraine Shaw before he went home, but both were out. Lorraine's mother, an older, plumper but less self-assured version of her daughter, said worriedly, 'I can't rightly say where you'll find them—Donovan's, maybe, they go there Mondays for the Happy Hour—but they might have gone somewhere like Rockerfellers instead. I'll give her a message, if you want, when she comes in.' And Morrissey had to be content with that. If her daughter got the message, she and Malcolm would be in his office early; if not, he would have to go and find them both.

The underpass where the muggings had taken place lay beneath a large roundabout at the south end of Malminster where four busy roads met. The centre of the roundabout had been cut out and its sloping sides landscaped, letting four pedestrian tunnels emerge briefly into daylight. Thoughtfully the council had provided wooden bench seats for any citizen who wanted to sit surrounded by traffic noise and a fug of carbon monoxide.

Morrissey parked on a side street and walked down the subway steps. There was a stale smell of urine, and several of the overhead lights were out. He went as far as the centre and stood for a minute looking up at the night sky, wondering why Mike should have been there at all. It wasn't on his way home or even near Fisher Comprehensive.

Then he remembered it was very near an amusement arcade that attracted a lot of complaints. Had Mike gone there to waste time, knowing that his mother would be waiting to go to the hospital?

He went back up the subway steps to his car, and because he was at that end of town, drove home through the back streets that took him along Eskdale Road and past the middle school. He was driving slowly on dipped headlights when he saw the boys climbing over the gate from the school yard and remembered Matthew Haines's complaint about graffiti. Because it was a dark car and not the white of a police Panda they took no notice, moving off without undue haste, their voices loud against the quiet night. He drove past them to stop at the first of the houses, and when they came near enough, grabbed the pair of them.

Handcuffed and in the back of the car, they were silent. Not until they were at the police station and the custody officer told them to turn out their pockets did he see, beside the cans of spray paint, Mike's wristwatch.

MARGARET SAID, 'Mike's going to be so pleased. I told him you'd find them in no time flat, but he was very depressed.'

Her husband hung his jacket over the back of a kitchen chair, seeing the clock hands were at eleven.

One day he'd be home when he promised; the miracle was that Margaret didn't object more frequently. He went to wash his hands at the sink. 'What was Mike doing in the underpass in the first place?' he said gruffly. 'It's not on his way home. Had you sent him on an errand?'

He heard the oven door open and the soft thud of the casserole on its wooden trivet, and knew Margaret was anxiously trying to think of a way to deflect his anger from Mike. That itself was a pointer to his son's guilt. But Morrissey *was* angry. Mike knew to keep away from that particular amusement arcade.

Margaret said, 'Getting angry with him won't help; the problem is what happened to Katie. He still believed having a policeman for a father would stop anything bad happening to us, and now he's had to face being wrong. I'm sorry, John. He's just lost faith in Superdad, and he's rebelling. Perhaps he'll get a bit of it back tomorrow when he knows you caught those two. Anyway, you can't talk to him tonight; he's asleep, and he's hurt.'

And so was Katie. Superdad! The chief inspector began to eat. Whatever Mike's reasons, he still had to be spoken to, reminded that being in the wrong place at the wrong time was avoidable. But Mike wouldn't like to be reminded, would see it as preaching, curtailing his freedom. He wondered if this would mark the beginning of a gulf between himself and his son. The idea was abhorrent, and his mind moved away from that and remembered another fear instead. He said, 'Can you remember who passed by when you washed the car this morning?'

She looked surprised. 'Walking?'

'Or driving.' He ate and waited, debated briefly whether to tell her about the telephone call, and accepted that he must.

'I suppose you want to know if I've rumbled your spy network,' she said. 'Who told you, anyway?' Then she saw his seriousness and made herself think back. 'I said hello to half a dozen neighbours, and at least twenty cars went past, including a police car. Then there were a couple of buses, an ice-cream van, the bin-men came, the postman brought a bill ... I don't remember anyone else. I'm sorry, John, but there could have been fifty people on the buses who saw me washing the car, and I wasn't looking all the time. It's hard to see everything that passes when you're sloshing water around. Are you going to tell me what it's about?'

When he told her, she met his eyes, and shrugged. 'I'm not worried,' she said. 'I know damn well you wouldn't let anything else happen,' and hoped he wouldn't recognise it as a lie.

THERE WAS a message on Morrissey's desk to say that Livesey and his girlfriend would come and see him at twelve-thirty. It wasn't what he wanted, but it would have to do. Just before half-past eight Peter Heslop came in to make a statement, needing to be reassured once again that it wouldn't directly hurt Mark.

Soon after Heslop left, Barrett went in search of Mandy Walters again. The previous night's effort had drawn a blank. The flat she once shared across the landing from Diane Anderson had been let to two nurses who knew nothing about her or her boyfriend, and no one else in the house could say where she had gone. Hicks's initial report gave her occupation as hairdresser, and Barrett hoped she was still in the same job.

For Morrissey, there had been a second message on his desk; this one demanding he be available to see Osgodby, upstairs, at nine. Morrissey guessed that his head on a plate would do equally well. But he was lucky, because before nine, news came in from forensic that not even the CC could shrug off. He debated with himself on the merits of a social system that made someone you played golf with less likely to commit murder than the man who brought the milk.

The new reports confirmed that Natalie Parkes had lain in the boot of her own car until she was dumped in the cemetery. There were fibres from her clothing and hairs from her head. But there were no fingerprints; Harding had been careful about that. What he hadn't been careful about were short grey hairs that clung to the driver's headrest and matched exactly hairs from his comb.

Taken by themselves, Harding might have explained them away, but he wouldn't be able to explain how another of those hairs came to be held fast in the knot of the strangulation cord. Content, Morrissey took the evidence for Osgodby to see.

The chief superintendent's sleepless night showed badly. Since Harding's arrest, he had been under pressure not to hold the editor unless there was more proof than suspicion, and he'd known there was virtually none. All he had to go on was Morrissey's instinct, and it had worried him. Now he read Peter Heslop's statement and saw the forensic reports, and knew his neck was safe.

'When you charge him,' he said grimly, 'I want to be there.'

And Morrissey nodded and knew that, for once, they were on the same wavelength.

THIRTY

THE STALE, sour, smell had permeated the flat for so long that he had grown used to it. It didn't come from any one source but gathered and hung in the air like a noxious miasma; some came from the grey-brown water in the sink that hid all the crockery he owned, some from the crusted WC, some from a stinking rag that he'd wiped up vomit with the night before and then thrown in a bucket that already held at least two more.

He had drunk too much, and his wallet was about empty. He swallowed the last four Paracetamols and through the throbbing headache tried to remember why he'd been celebrating. When his head cleared, he remembered the joke he'd played on Morrissey, and started laughing again.

That bloody dosser had been kipping out down the wharf for weeks, picking up dog-ends, scavenging food.

As the pain eased in his skull, he savoured the cleverness of aping the man. That it could have been a mistake didn't enter his head, neither did the idea that Morrissey might be drawing closer to him. Instead, his mind concentrated itself on the plaited garrotte in his pocket and the pleasure it would bring him.

His mind licked around the bitch who had started it all. If he knew where to find her, he would slide it over her throat. He hadn't even hit her that hard, nowhere near as hard as he'd hit the bitch in Bolton. There'd been no call to go screaming to Diane. He'd shouted at her to come back; but she'd yelled, loud enough for all the house to hear, *'Get lost, Foxy, get lost. You're a psycho!'*

Three dead bitches. When they found out it was her fault, *they'd lock her up for good*.

Walking to work, he expected to see police activity along the wharf, when he didn't, he felt disappointment, and his hand sought comfort from the twine in his pocket. All there was inside him, all there had ever been, was twisting anger, cold and dispassionate as a ball of ice.

THIRTY-ONE

HARDING DREW the wrong conclusion when he saw Osgodby in the interview room. He believed Morrissey was about to be overruled, and the thought of walking out free and leaving the chief inspector looking a fool was enjoyable. Fred Burridge was with them.

'It's about bloody time!' Harding said. 'Get it over with and let me get home.' Confident, he thrust out his chin. Without preamble, Morrissey formally charged him with the murder of Natalie Parkes, and saw the confidence turn into something more primitive.

Burridge, with distant detachment, said, 'I'd recommend Jameson as defence lawyer. Do you want me to brief him?'

'Brief who you bloody well want!' Harding shouted. The veins in his forehead stood in thin ropes. 'Bloody get me out of here!' In his anger, he lifted one of the squat wooden chairs and smashed it on the table.

It was an instinctive reactive violence that Morrissey understood without condoning, and reason had no place in it. If Harding had killed in that kind of anger, a jury might even have seen it as human, but he hadn't; the twine had been knotted and ready for Natalie's throat when he went to meet her.

And in that detail alone he had done what he set out to do and duplicated the mind of the serial killer.

IT TOOK Barrett almost the whole morning to locate Mandy Walters. He'd gone to the salon where she had worked as a stylist and found she had given up her hairdressing job the day after Hicks had been called to her flat. She hadn't told the other girls where she was going, and they were aggrieved not to be confided in.

But, as one of them admitted, they could understand why. 'That feller she'd been living with was a nut-case,' the girl said. 'We'd been on at her for months to dump him. Mandy didn't dare keep working here in case he came round looking for her when they split.'

'And did he?' asked Barrett.

'Every day for about a month. Hanging about outside and looking through the window all the time; off-putting, if you know what I mean. Then he stopped.'

'You must have known his name, then?'

'Foxy. That's all Mandy ever called him. Not bad-looking, I suppose, if you like that type.'

'What type?'

There was a ripple of amusement. 'Sort of cross between John Travolta and Jack the Ripper. Mandy said he had a drinking problem, and it'd got so bad he couldn't get it up unless he knocked her about first.' She grinned at Barrett, and said archly, 'Bet you don't have problems like that.'

He thought about his erratic love life and left her to speculate.

When he finally found Mandy, it was through the housing agency who had rented her the flat. Only her name was on the agreement; Foxy had obviously been a later unofficial addition. Before that, according to the file, she'd lived with her parents in Inchwood, eight miles away.

When the detective sergeant walked up the front path of the neat colliery house, he found her father blocking his way. Only when Barrett produced his warrant card did the man let his spade slide back into the newly-dug soil, and lead the way round to the kitchen door.

His first glance at her told Barrett why Mandy had gone home. In the bulky maternity dress she looked awkwardly unbalanced, and he knew the baby couldn't be more than a couple of months away. Having intended to be brusque, to bully information from her if she wouldn't give it easily, he had to change to a gentler stance, and it didn't come easily. He tried to think how Morrissey would handle it.

'Sit down,' he said. 'It isn't anything to do with you personally; nothing for you to worry about. I'm looking for Foxy. Do you know where he's living since you split up?'

'No,' the girl said. 'I don't even want to know. What do you want him for?'

'We need to talk to all the men who knew Diane Anderson before she died. Foxy knew her, didn't he?'

Mandy said, 'Only because she took me into her place when he was hitting me that last time. He'd only seen her on the stairs before that.'

'It was Diane who called the police?'

'Yes.'

'And you stayed in her flat all that night?' She nodded. He said, 'Did you see her after you moved out of your place?'

'Just once, when we bumped into each other in Malminster market. We went for a cup of tea, and she said she'd had problems with him after I left; he'd been round banging on her door.' Feeling for the chair behind her, she flopped down heavily. 'Then I found out she'd been killed. I couldn't believe it! I wish it had been somebody else.'

'Our Mandy thought it might have been him, until it came out it were t'same bugger who'd killed that other lass,' her father said. 'But I'll tell you this: I've never hit my women, and I'm not letting any other bastard start! If he comes round here, I'll have him.'

Unless he and Morrissey had him first, thought Barrett, and asked for Foxy's full name.

'Vincent Darryl Fox. He works for Plumley's.' Mandy rested her hands on the bulge. 'I can't stand the thought of it turning out like him. I hope it's a girl.' There was desperation. 'It *has* to be a girl!'

IN MORRISSEY'S OFFICE, the young couple were surprised. The chief inspector had let them see the photograph of themselves buying ice-cream.

'I didn't think that was anything you'd be interested in,' Malcolm Livesey admitted. 'Lorraine wanted me to stop him. I didn't think he would, at first, he was going at a fair old pace.'

'Well, he did,' said Lorraine. 'It was Plumley's, you see, or I wouldn't have bothered,' she explained. 'They use real cream, not that substitute white stuff.'

'I know,' said Morrissey. 'Worth going out of your way for. But I wish you'd told me about it before; I did ask for everyone you'd seen.'

'Well yes, but he was after it happened, wasn't he? We didn't think he mattered.'

'He might matter very much,' the chief inspector said severely.

Lorraine said, 'Well, he definitely had something on his mind.'

'You don't know that,' Malcolm quibbled, and she took on a stubborn look that told Morrissey they were travelling over old ground.

The chief inspector said, 'What makes you say that? Something odd about him, was there, or was it just the speed he was doing?'

'Odd,' she said. 'I mean, why wear washing-up gloves to drive in, for a start?'

'To keep his hands clean,' Malcolm said shortly. 'We've been through this before.'

Morrissey tried not to betray sudden interest. 'What colour were they?'

'Yellow.'

'And did he take them off to serve you?'

'Yes. But he didn't put them back on when he drove off, so they weren't to keep his hands clean, were they?' she said, proving her point triumphantly.

Malcolm sighed and rolled his eyes to the ceiling.

'Describe him for me,' said Morrissey. 'Best you can. Young, was he?'

'Bit like John Travolta,' she said. 'Don't you think so, Mal?'

'Foxyish, that's what I'd say. Shifty with it.'

'But he put plenty of ice-cream in,' Lorraine said. 'You've got to be fair, haven't you?'

'Yes,' said Morrissey. 'You've got to be fair.'

COMING BACK INTO the building at a trot, Barrett passed Lorraine and Malcolm on the steps; they appeared to be having a minor row and didn't seem to notice him.

Anxious to report what he'd unearthed, he took the stairs too rapidly and was puffing when he went into the office and saw Morrissey.

'I found Mandy...' he began.

The chief inspector had more on his mind than an old domestic dispute. Whatever Barrett wanted to say would have to wait. He said bluntly, 'We might have him, Neil. One of Plumley's van-drivers. What we want now is a name.'

Barrett took on an air of omnipotence. 'Vincent Darryl Fox,' he said with satisfaction. He smiled beatifically. 'Mandy Walters's cohabitee. That's what I was trying to tell you.'

THIRTY-TWO

GEOFF CARTER managed the ice-cream side of Plumley's Dairy. A bone thin and worried-looking man with sandy hair receding like his chin, the last thing he needed right then was trouble with the police; not right on top of a visit from the council's Environmental Health officer. How the hell was he supposed to stop rats coming up from the wharf? From his office at the back of the dairy yard where he could watch the vans come and go, he'd seen Morrissey drive in with a couple of Pandas behind, and it had worried him. He gave the chief inspector a fretful look.

'I didn't know he'd dropped in any bother or I wouldn't have kept him on,' he said. 'What's he been up to?' He handed Morrissey a wages card marked Fox, V.D. 'Nothing bad, is it?'

Morrissey glanced at it, and said, 'Does he keep to the same area every day, round by the common?'

'Not always. He hasn't got it today, for a start. Truth is, I didn't think he was up to driving. He gets a bit of a skinful some nights, so if he looks hung over I usually put him in one of the stationaries. He's near the park gates today, by the tennis courts.'

'You'll keep records, though, where your drivers go each day? Need to, I should think.'

'They keep log-books; have to for petrol and mileage and that.'

Barrett said, 'I'd like a look at Foxy's.'

Carter picked up a brown-backed duplicate book, and Barrett reached for it with a sense of things winding up. He turned back through the pages looking for the dates he wanted.

Morrissey said, 'What's he like, then, Foxy? Been with you a long time?'

'He's got his problems,' Carter said. 'Haven't we all? Not that likeable, I suppose. Some of the lads say he's a nutter, but he didn't have a right good start. He's worked here eighteen months or so, and he's given me no bother.'

'You knew him before that?' Morrissey said sharply.

'Lived round the corner from me when he was a kid, poor sod. Remember the back-to-backs where they built the skate park? Him and his ma, just the two of them, third house down on Garden Street.'

'No father?'

'Well, we all have, don't we? Be hard for him to know his.' He caught Morrissey's frown, and said, 'You'll have met up with his mother—she worked the pubs round Market Place. Hard-faced twat.' Barrett looked up from the log.

Morrissey said, 'She was a prostitute?'

'Two-a-time Tina.' He saw knowledge flick into the chief inspector's eyes, and said, 'I thought that'd ring a bell! Had him pimping nearly as soon as he could talk.'

Tina Haigh. Morrissey blinked. He'd booked her for trawling half a dozen times. He said. 'Where is she now? Foxy supporting her, is he?'

'Never saw her after they pulled the houses down. Foxy moved up to Bolton for a bit, but he's in a flat on his own now—right pigsty. You've got the address on his wages card.'

'So I have,' said Morrissey. His eyes went to Barrett, and saw him pat the log and nod. 'I'm grateful for your help,' he told Carter, and moved out of the office and to his car in long strides.

Carter watched them go, thinking that if the van had a phone, he'd let Foxy know they were looking for him.

He wondered vaguely what the ice-cream salesman had done. If it was theft, he'd need to find out; he might be able to turn a blind eye to some things, but not sticky fingers. Making a note to remind himself to question Foxy when he came in, he plugged in the kettle and went back to balancing the cash-book.

FOXY'S DAY had started badly, and not improved. He didn't like being stuck in a stationary; he'd wanted to be on the road, watching out for likely places. The weather had started sunny, but by mid-morning thin high cloud had drifted in from the east, bringing with it a cold snickering breeze, and the park was almost deserted.

Except for a brief flurry of trade at mid-day, mostly from the comprehensive school on the far side of the park, Foxy was wasting his time, and cursing about it. The fish and chip shop across the road was a better attraction for tuck-money.

The young teenagers had all wandered back up the hill now, except for one girl who had a boyfriend at a quick-fit tyre place next to the fish and chip shop. Those two had been arguing for a good ten minutes, and Foxy was hanging with his head out of the van to watch. Neither gave him a glance, and the traffic noise made it impossible to hear what they were saying. But he caught the last bit, because the girl raised her voice.

'Get lost!'

Foxy withdrew his head and watched from inside as she waited to cross the road. Like Mandy, her hair was blond, and it had been cut in the same style, long on top and short at the sides and back. He'd liked to rub his fingers up the short hairs. She'd liked it, too; it'd been a turn-on before she'd gone whingeing to Diane.

Get lost. She'd said it to *him*.

Women were dirt. He felt in his trouser pocket and, touching the plaited twine, was reassured.

The sixth-former walked with her head bent and didn't look at him as she went past. When she reached the path between the tennis courts and pitch 'n' putt, he locked the van and followed. She shouldn't have made herself look like Mandy; it was asking for it.

The van was still locked when Morrissey and Barrett came into the park, not knowing they'd missed Foxy by only a few minutes. The chief inspector felt unease; not only because the van was empty but from something more intangible that seemed to bring the hairs behind his neck upright. There were three other exits to the park, and he'd sent a patrol car to each. He glanced over his shoulder to where Copeland and Smythe waited for his signal.

'He could have gone for a leak,' Barrett suggested. 'Bit awkward, in there all day.'

Morrissey said, 'It's too quiet. Take out the traffic noise, and there's nothing.' His disquiet communicated itself, and Barrett turned, listening. 'No birds,' Morrissey said. 'Not a chirrup.'

Barrett wagged his fingers at the DCs. 'Might as well have them look in the john,' he said uneasily. 'No point standing there doing nothing. Foxy'll have had his little rush of customers and gone for a pee.'

Morrissey said. 'What rush?'

'Park Comp. Unless things have changed, they come down here in hordes to the chippy, and if they've enough left, they get a lolly on their way back.'

Morrissey swung round to look at the asphalt path that bisected the park, wide enough for cycling but not meant for driving on. His eyes followed it up the rise to the crest of the pitch 'n' putt where the tops of rhododendrons showed. On the right, a line of trees marched towards the walled rose garden.

A flight of starlings lifted up, noisy and chattering. 'Something's disturbed them,' Barrett said.

But Morrissey was already breaking into a run as he headed for the circling birds, his long limbs ungainly, his vented jacket flapping. Over his shoulder, he roared, 'He's got another! *Move* it, for God's sake!'

And they moved, panicking.

Foxy was among the rhododendrons straddling the girl, the twine tight in his hands. This time, the exhilaration was tremendous, and his mind sang with the power that went through his hands, and the pounding of Morrissey's feet mingled with the pounding of blood in his head, and until the large hands closed and lifted him upright he didn't know the chief inspector was there.

KATIE HAD BEEN home a week, and Malminster was getting itself back to normal again. The sixth-former had been lucky, and Morrissey hoped she would remember to be kind to birds.

He knew that chance had played a large part in the investigation: if Hicks hadn't seen the computer printout and made the link between Foxy and Diane, it would have taken longer, but that's what police work was about. Every case, when you came right down to it, was nine parts detection and one part chance. Like the Yorkshire Ripper being caught over a motoring offence.

But the real thanks went to Colin and his camera, and Morrissey didn't intend to forget that, or to let the Division forget it, either. It was amazing how people reached in their pockets with the right pressure. CID had already held their own celebration party; next week they were going to give Colin his. He'd enjoy a ride in a Panda with the siren going, and a VIP tour of operations, and he'd probably like going round the photo lab even more. And when he'd had his celebration tea, Osgodby, dressed up in his best, would hand over the coveted enlarger with all their thanks. It was something the chief inspector was looking forward to.

Barrett was also looking forward to something. He was cockahoop because he had two tickets for *Cats*, and he was taking Michelle. It meant an overnight stay in London, and he was looking forward to that, too.

'Separate rooms, I hope,' said the chief inspector severely, and put on an intimidating face.

Barrett grinned. He was still grinning when Janet Yarby came in with a file of papers for him. She saw the tickets on his desk, and picked them up.

'I'd give an arm and a leg to see the London production,' she said, and put them back regretfully. 'But it's no good thinking about it. I know you don't

have one spare.' With a sad little smile, she turned
away from him and grinned broadly at Morrissey.
Everyone in the station knew he was taking Michelle, but it didn't hurt to turn the screw.

Barrett put the tickets in his wallet and thought
about his long-standing pursuit of Janet. He stared at
the closed door dolefully.

'It's always painful,' Morrissey pointed out, 'trying to ride two horses.' And with an unsympathetic
leer he went home.

There were voices coming from the kitchen: Margaret's and Katie's. He hung his jacket on the hall
stand and, walking towards the sound, heard a third
voice.

One of Katie's boyfriends, no doubt. Bees round a
honey-pot. But he was glad she brought them home;
her trust showed that they hadn't altogether failed as
parents. And what if she brought someone unsuit-
able? Well. It was easier to work from inside than
nibble at distant edges. He shrugged off the gloomy
thought; Katie was wise enough.

Morrissey thrust open the kitchen door.

Hicks was wearing a T-shirt that bade the chief inspector *Save the Forests*. He saw Morrissey, and went
red. 'Sir.'

Morrissey glowered. 'What wouldn't wait, Hicks?'
he asked tersely. Katie shot him an odd look, and
grabbed the young PC's rigid hand.

Margaret smiled brightly. 'Katie brought Ian home for a meal before they go on to a disco,' she said. 'Isn't that nice?'

'Wonderful!' said Morrissey, giving the young man a tiger's smile, and went upstairs to change.

Death DOWN HOME

EVE K. SANDSTROM

A SAM AND NICKY TITUS MYSTERY

First Time in Paperback

MURDER IS A FAMILY AFFAIR

Reality was a far cry from the posthoneymoon bliss Nicky Titus envisioned. First came the frantic call, then the flight from Frankfurt, and finally the arrival of Sam and Nicky down home in Holton, Oklahoma, where Sam's father, big Sam, lay in a coma after an "accident" on the ranch.

Convinced that somebody had tried to kill his father, young Sam Titus plunges into his own investigation and soon it's clear that no one in the Titus family is safe—not even its newest member, Nicky!

"A crackerjack new series."

—*Kirkus Reviews*

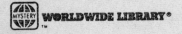
DEATH

A SUSAN WREN MYSTERY

THE WINTER WIDOW

CHARLENE WEIR

First Time in Paperback

SHE'D BEEN ONE OF SAN FRANCISCO'S FINEST—SEMI-HARD-BITTEN, CYNICAL AND HAPPILY UNATTACHED...

Until Daniel Wren blew in like a tornado, sweeping Susan off her feet and back home to Hampstead, Kansas, new bride of the small town's police chief. Ten days later Daniel was killed by a sniper.

Susan was an outsider—a city slicker, a woman, and worse, personally involved in the case. She was also Hampstead's new police chief... hunting for her husband's killer.

"Nonstop action and harrowing suspense." —*Publishers Weekly*

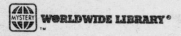

MYSTERY **WORLDWIDE LIBRARY**®
TM

WIDOW

CHASING AWAY THE DEVIL

A MILT KOVAK MYSTERY

First Time in Paperback

SUSAN ROGERS COOPER

HEAVEN CAN WAIT

On Friday night, Sheriff Milt Kovak of Prophesy County, Oklahoma, proposed to his longtime ladylove, Glenda Sue. She turned him down. On Saturday morning, Glenda Sue is found brutally murdered.

Kovak begins a desperate search to find the killer, well aware he's a suspect himself. When he discovers a first-class, one-way ticket to Paris in Glenda Sue's belongings, it's pretty clear she had been keeping secrets—deadly secrets.

"Milt is a delightful narrator, both bemused and acerbic."
—*Publishers Weekly*

Available in October at your favorite retail stores.

To reserve your copy for September shipping, please send your name, address, zip or postal code, along with a check or money order for $3.99 (please do not send cash), plus 75¢ postage and handling ($1.00 in Canada) for each book ordered, payable to Worldwide Mystery, to:

In the U.S.

Worldwide Mystery
3010 Walden Avenue
P.O. Box 1325
Buffalo, NY 14269-1325

In Canada

Worldwide Mystery
P.O. Box 609
Fort Erie, Ontario
L2A 5X3

Please specify book title with your order.
Canadian residents add applicable federal and provincial taxes.

DEVIL

MYSTERY **WORLDWIDE LIBRARY** ®

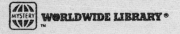